"Relax, Jack, it was just a kiss."

Laura's voice sounded confident and steady. Did he think she was still a sixteen-year-old who couldn't handle a kiss without falling in love? "Really," she said to his rapidly flushing face, "it's no big deal."

She smiled, watching his ego deflate. "I'll see you tomorrow."

It was only after she'd started the van and was on her way back home that she realized she had just told Jack she wasn't quitting. It was one thing to brazen it out for a couple of minutes, but she couldn't keep up the act for long. She felt just like a lovesick teenager again.

Maybe worse.

Laura banged her fist on the steering wheel. "Stupid, stupid, stupid." She'd backed herself into a tight corner, but she was an expert at avoiding intimacy. All she had to do was make sure she and the sexy carpenter worked in different parts of the house.

Dear Reader,

When the phone rang with the news that I had won Harlequin's Blaze Contest, I was thrilled. When it rang again, two weeks later, with the news that Harlequin was going to publish three of my books, I just about had a heart attack!

Flashback is the first of these. Interior designer Laura Kincaide isn't exactly thrilled when she finds out she'll be working with the sexy carpenter who dumped her in high school. But it's amazing what a difference the years have made. Now he wants her back; but it's a very adult relationship he has in mind. When the words, emotions and the paint start to fly—watch out!

I hope you have as much fun reading *Flashback* as I had writing it. Please watch for my next books— *Live a Little,* a steamy read for the new Harlequin Blaze line, and *Shotgun Nanny,* a Harlequin Duets title.

Regards,

Nancy Warren

FLASHBACK
Nancy Warren

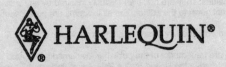

HARLEQUIN®

TORONTO • NEW YORK • LONDON
AMSTERDAM • PARIS • SYDNEY • HAMBURG
STOCKHOLM • ATHENS • TOKYO • MILAN • MADRID
PRAGUE • WARSAW • BUDAPEST • AUCKLAND

I wouldn't have become a writer
without the love and support of my parents,
Pat and Harry Weatherley.
Thanks also to my three Graces: editors
Susan Sheppard, Birgit Davis-Todd and Brenda Chin.

ISBN 0-373-25938-7

FLASHBACK

Copyright © 2001 by Nancy Warren.

1

"YOU HAVE A PROBLEM with intimacy, Laura."

Laura Kinkaide rolled her gaze to the stained ceiling. "Stan, I need furniture wax, not a lecture on my defective psyche." As if Stan Stukowsky with his thirty-year marriage had any idea what it was like to be single these days.

Stan shook his bald head, clinking through cans and tubes on cluttered, grimy shelves. "How long did—what was his name—this one last?"

"I dated Peter for about three months." Laura tapped her fingers on the goo-covered worktable. "Look, I just ran in to get the wax. I do not have time for this conversation. I'm trying to get the Gibsons' apartment finished today."

"My gosh, three whole months." Stan's voice sounded like a piece of steel going through a cheese grater. Giving up on that shelf, he bent to riffle through the lower shelves.

She took a slow, deep breath, refusing to rise to Stan's pop-psychology bait. The smells of paint, wax and ancient wood were as thick as the dust.

His muffled voice floated up to her. "How long did you go out with the guy before him?"

She knew where this was going. "Twelve weeks."

"And the one before that?"

Laura glared at Stan's back. If he wasn't the best supplier she knew, she really wouldn't put up with him. She enunciated each word slowly: "A quarter of a year."

"No matter how you say it, darlin', it's still three months. Walnut or pine?"

"What?"

"The furniture polish. What's it for?" Stan asked, rising with a squat can in each hand.

"Oh." Laura had to think. "I've done a pale-green crackle finish on the armoire in the bedroom. I want to give it an antique patina."

He nodded, handing her the walnut. "What's up after the Gibson place?"

She rolled aching shoulders. "A vacation."

"So, why'd you dump him?"

Oh, God. He was back to that again, was he? "How do you know I dumped him? Maybe he dumped me."

Stan just gazed at her with his I've-known-you-for-ten-years-don't-give-me-that look.

Laura sighed noisily, trying not to look defensive. "He bites his nails."

Stan nodded, as though she'd said just what he expected. "You dump a perfectly good guy with a thriving law practice because he bites his nails. And you don't think you have an intimacy problem?"

"I hardly think you're qualified to judge, Stan. The last time *you* had a date, the Beatles were together. Chocolate bars cost a nickel. And—" she gestured to the damaged treasures that littered his workroom like an upmarket garage sale "—most of this stuff was brand-new. Believe me, times have changed."

"So now you're taking another vacation alone?"

Sounds drifted back from the front shop of Vintage Restorations, where Stan's wife sold stencils, specialty paints and books for do-it-yourself decorators. Laura heard the hum of voices, along with the odd burst of laughter and the regular ringing of the till.

"What kind of vacation would I have with a guy chomping his nails in my ear? Women are independent these days. We do things for ourselves and by ourselves."

"Laura, I've had hangovers that lasted longer than some of your relationships. The way you're going you'll run through every unattached male in Seattle before Christmas."

She narrowed her eyes. "Are you calling me a slut?"

Stan's guffaw puffed a dust cloud off his worktable. "If you had sex with these guys more often, you might not notice that they bite their nails, or watch the wrong movies or make corny jokes." He leaned forward and patted her hand. "You'll never find a perfect man. You're just making excuses to avoid intimacy."

"I get plenty of sex, thank you," Laura retorted, her voice raised in annoyance.

"Lucky you," a rich baritone drawled behind her right shoulder.

She saw her own horror reflected in Stan's eyes, felt the blood rising, flushing up her neck, hitting her face like a volcanic eruption. She and Stan had been alone. How had a strange man sneaked up on them?

A man with that voice.

A deep, sexy voice that set off an answering quiver

somewhere inside her chest. There was only one person who'd ever been able to do that to her.

He'd spoken only two words. It couldn't be Jack. Please, let it be a stranger who'd overheard them talking about her pitiful sex life. Let it be anyone but Jack. She turned slowly....

"Hello, Laura."

"Jack..."

For just a second she was a lovesick teenager again, looking up into the face of her hero. Then she saw the changes time had wrought.

Years and experience had added hard edges to the boy she'd once loved. His eyes were just as blue, but now they had a few crinkly lines around their corners, while that wavy blond hair had darkened to a rich ash. He had the same tall athlete's body, but his chest seemed wider, his shoulders broader, and he held himself with a new assurance. Everything about him had matured and filled out except his lips, which looked a little thinner, as though he didn't laugh as much as he used to.

She realized she was staring, and glanced away. "What are you doing here?" Her voice sounded raspy. Her heart was jumping all around her rib cage like a flipped-out canary.

"Your grandmother asked me to drop this off. She said you get mail at this store." He held out a large brown envelope. "The lady out front sent me back here."

He was looking down at her in a way that made Laura wish she'd consulted a mirror recently. She was pretty sure she had pale-green paint spattered all over her—it was certainly splotched all over the hand that moved reluctantly forward to take the package. She probably looked in need of major restoration— right at home with all the other disasters in Stan's workshop.

"Why didn't she just mail it?" Or at least warn Laura he was coming.

He shrugged, his denim shirt moving up and down over sturdy shoulders. "She wanted you to get it fast, I guess. I happened to be coming to Seattle." His eyes crinkled. "And you know how she likes to save a penny."

Laura felt herself smiling back. They had so much history together. Jack knew Gran almost as well as she did, knew she hated waste of any kind—wasted money most of all.

Laura took the package from Jack's outstretched hand, trying not to notice how strong and capable that hand looked. The nails, she noted, were short and neatly trimmed, not bitten. Quickly, she shifted her attention to the envelope. "Thanks for bringing it."

Laura felt Stan's inquisitive little eyes darting back and forth between her and Jack, sensed him sniffing the atmosphere like a French sow nosing the dirt for truffles. Really, if she didn't love him like a second father, the man would drive her crazy. She introduced them. "Stan Stukowsky, Jack Thomas."

The men shook hands, sizing each other up. Jack was a head taller than the older man. He stood confidently at ease, weight evenly distributed on long legs. Energy seemed to radiate from him.

"Laura and I grew up together on Whidbey Island," Jack said.

"Well, any friend of—"

She interrupted, "We're not..."

"We haven't seen each other in a while," Jack finished. "Laura doesn't get back to Laroche much." He glanced at her then. Could she be reading recrimination in his gaze? When he was the reason she'd left home in the first place?

"Must be important if your grandmother wanted it delivered personally." Stan nodded his head at the envelope. Did he think he was being subtle? Well, he could die of old age waiting for her to open the package. Knowing Gran, she'd probably signed Laura up with one of those dating services.

She shrugged. "It's probably stock tips. Gran has a lot of time to read, so she keeps me up to date on the markets."

"Your gran tells me you're pretty successful." Jack leaned against the workbench at Laura's side, close enough that she felt his warmth. His chest was at eye level and a swirl of coppery hair in the vee of his open shirt snagged her attention. She quickly forced her gaze to the floor.

"I do okay."

"Laura's the best designer and restorer of Victorian interiors in the business," Stan announced with avuncular pride.

"I keep telling her to hire staff, but she says she can only keep her quality top-notch if she does the work herself."

She'd never noticed how much wax and oil there was caked on the floor. The place was an absolute fire hazard. She scraped at an amber glob with her toe.

"Isn't that mirror a Chippendale?" Jack asked.

Laura glanced up. Football, Jack Thomas knew about, but furniture styles? She'd have guessed *he* would define Chippendale as a male stripper. Or a couple of Disney characters. Not that he could have unerringly spotted the masterpiece in Stan's current collection.

"We can't authenticate it," Stan said. He worked his way over to where the mirror lay atop a marble commode, and carried it back carefully. "I picked it up at auction to restore and sell, but..." He shrugged massive shoulders. "I think I'll keep it myself." He couldn't disguise the note of smug pride in his tone.

Jack nodded, caressing the ancient frame. "It's a beauty." In the wavering reflection, she witnessed his intensity as he ran his long fingers over the scarred wood, as if it were a lover's face.

She couldn't tear her gaze away. Their eyes locked for a moment in the speckled mirror. Their images seemed oddly distorted.

Laura forgot to breathe. She'd outgrown her teenage infatuation with Jack along with her Barbie dolls and training bras. She just wished that, after all these years, she didn't feel such a sense of connection with him.

"Are you in the business?" Stan's voice broke the spell and Laura breathed again. A sharp, jerky pant.

"I'm a carpenter." Jack shrugged, his reflected gaze still on Laura. "I've picked up a little knowledge here and there." There was another pause, during which she waited for him to continue. But all he said was, "Well, good to see you again, Laura. Nice to meet you, Stan."

Jack lifted his hand in a casual gesture and sauntered out.

Unable to help herself, she watched his broad back as he walked away with an athlete's ease and confidence. And God, she loved men in well-worn blue jeans. She realized she was leaning heavily against the worktable, and had a feeling it was the only thing holding her up. Damn it, how could Jack still affect her?

Stan hadn't missed her reaction. He was almost rubbing his hands with glee, planning Peter's replacement. "He seemed—"

"You'll be pleased to know that *he* dumped *me!*"

Stan's eyes widened. "I don't remember a Jack... should I?"

Laura felt herself beginning to blush all over again. "It happened when I was sixteen." She shrugged. "We went out for a while and then he dumped me. It's no big deal."

Stan lit up like Freud after a cigar-laden dream. "Ah-ha!" he cried, throwing both hands in the air.

LAURA RUBBED her cramped biceps with a groan. She lay collapsed on the couch in her apartment, too tired even to take a shower. The Gibsons' armoire now wore the patina of a Renaissance painting, but hard as she'd rubbed the dark polish into the crackled paint, she couldn't erase the humiliating scene in Stan's workshop from her memory.

It was almost twelve years since she'd stood that close to Jack, since they'd exchanged more than the skimpiest casual greeting in passing. And he had to find her in stained overalls, her hair a mess, paint spattered God-knows-where, while Stan told her she wasn't getting enough sex.

It wasn't one of her better days.

Although the day had improved when she'd placed her elegant gilt-edged envelope on the Gibsons' gleaming dining table. It contained her final bill—an amount large enough to finance a decent holiday.

There was nothing elegant about the thick brown envelope Jack had delivered from Gran. Since her grandmother's light reading had started to include the *Financial Times* and *Barron's*, she'd often sent Laura advice and snipped-out articles. And because Laura couldn't bear to think of all that work going to waste, she even followed Gran's advice occasionally, putting small sums of money into the stocks and other investments her grandmother recommended.

It had started out as a kind of charity, but darn it, her white-haired gran had been right about a lot of things. Laura's profit on Microsoft alone had paid for her current computer.

Wondering whether it was pork bellies or another impotency drug Gran was touting, Laura ripped open the envelope, which crackled loudly in the silence of her apartment. Out slid a paper-clipped bundle of papers topped by an 8-by-10 photograph.

She raised the photo to study it more closely, and let out a soft sound of distress when she saw the run-down building.

Not her dream house!

Once a gracious Victorian home, the old house sagged with neglect. Most of the paint was cracked and peeling like decaying skin. The fine leaded windows were boarded up, the sparkling coquettish eyes rendered blind. Bits of gingerbread trim were missing;

lengths of lacy wrought-iron railing had disappeared. Moss hung lank from the turreted roof. You could almost smell the musty air inside. The duchess had become a bag lady.

Looking at the photo was like seeing a cherished friend seriously ill; it hurt Laura somewhere deep inside. She touched the picture fondly, outlining the shape of the house with a fingertip.

In the three years since she'd last visited her hometown on Whidbey Island, the house had really deteriorated. She still thought of it as "her house," the old McNair place that was so much a part of all her childish dreams.

She placed the photo on her lap and picked up the papers. The covering letter was written on the official stationery of the village of Laroche by the Sea.

Dear Ms. Kinkaide:

You have been recommended to the Save McNair House committee to help restore this historic landmark to its original condition. It is the wish of this committee to operate McNair House as a museum and tourist attraction commencing this upcoming summer season.

We invite you to submit a proposal to decorate the interior of the home, including supervising its furnishing, authentic to the period in which it was built (circa 1886).

Yours sincerely,
Dolores Walters (Mrs.)
Chairwoman, Save McNair House Committee

A bubble of excitement rose from deep inside. Laura grabbed the bundle of papers, flipped on her computer and elbowed a pile of vacation brochures onto the floor.

Within minutes she was on the phone.

"Hi, Stan, it's Laura. Do you still have some of that vintage flocked wall covering, the maroon? Great, hold on to it for me. I'm going to fax you a tentative supply list on a fabulous project I'm quoting, so give me your absolute best price on everything."

"I always do, darlin,'" said the gravelly voice on the other end. "Ah, what about your vacation?"

"This house is the project of a lifetime. It's going to be the best thing I've ever done. Besides, it's on beautiful Whidbey Island," she added breezily. "A perfect vacation spot."

"Whidbey? Is that what the package was about?"

"Yep."

"So, does the Heartbreak Kid still live there?"

"Don't even think about it, Stan. I'll be working on the house. I won't be seeing Jack Thomas."

Her next call was to Laroche.

"Why, Laura, what a nice surprise to hear from you," Gran's voice bellowed through the phone lines.

With a grimace, Laura pulled the phone a foot away from her ear. Gran always pitched her voice according to how far away the other person was. Laura had yet to convince her that telephones had improved since her girlhood. Long distance calls with her grandmother were deafening.

"That's a big fat lie if I ever heard one," she said into the receiver, resisting the temptation to shout back.

"You knew darn well I'd be calling. I saw your name on the Save the McNair committee list."

The old woman chuckled into the phone. "I'll get your room ready, dear. When do you start work?"

"I haven't been offered the contract yet."

"You will. I haven't lived in this town for eighty-two years for nothing. Why, I pulled down the mayor's pants and spanked him right on Main Street when I caught him stealing Mrs. Allen's apples." The old lady chuckled richly in reminiscence. "'Course, he wasn't the mayor then...."

"I'm sure he's reformed since he was seven years old, Gran," Laura teased. She was also sure he wouldn't ever go against her grandmother's wishes in case she told the story in public. "Do you know you can go to jail for blackmail?"

"Hmm. Stealing apples is a crime, too, young lady. Maybe our politicians in Laroche aren't as bad as some, but they've all got their dirty secrets. And I know all of them."

"I'll bet you do." Laura smiled, picturing that white-haired little old lady with the will of iron.

"You come down on Sunday, Laura. I'll cook a pot roast. You can start work Monday." There was a short pause, then Gran's voice dropped a decibel or two. "It's time you came home. We miss you."

2

LAURA SAT CROSS-LEGGED on the floor of the master bedroom in the McNair House, still amazed that her grandmother had pulled this off. Laura had received a contract—signed by the mayor—on her fax machine only a day after she'd faxed her proposal.

A blank sketching pad on her knee, she contemplated the huge mahogany four-poster bed that sat like deposed royalty against one wall of the run-down room, its ragged canopy drooping.

Morning sun streamed in through open windows, along with a cool spring breeze, but she was well bundled in a chunky sweater under her working overalls.

Even though it was dingy and decrepit, the room had gorgeous bones, with nine foot ceilings, a turret alcove, a Victorian fireplace—and that fantastic bed. There was no other furniture in the room, or much evidence of previous decorating. A few paper cabbage roses clung stubbornly to the walls, but the rest of the wallpaper had peeled off long ago.

The bed was obviously just too big to move. Laura spent a moment trying to figure out how anybody had ever got it in the room in the first place. To her mind both the doorway and the windows were way too small.

Whatever the reason, she was glad it had been left,

and not chopped up for firewood or something during the house's days of neglect. The bed was an excellent example of late nineteenth century American furniture, and it would hold pride of place in the completed room.

The bed and the roses... Images and ideas jostled each other in her mind until she was frantically sketching and scribbling. She taped pieces of the old wallpaper and bed canopy to her design sheet and began playing with color combinations.

When she noticed her bottom getting numb, she moved without conscious thought to the bed. The mattress smelled musty and bulged with lumps, but it held her weight. She lay down on it, squinting at the ragged material above her, trying to picture how the canopy would look if she could recreate the original fabric.

"Lounging on the job?" The deep, familiar voice was laced with teasing humor.

A shiver crept up her spine as she turned her head. "Is sneaking up on me in embarrassing situations a new and charming habit?" She made a mental note to get her ears checked.

There was a suggestion of a smile in Jack's eyes as he stood in the doorway, gazing down at her. "Welcome home."

She shouldn't have looked at him. That canary trapped in her rib cage was doing its thing again. It just wasn't fair that while lots of much nicer guys had lost their hair or got fat, Jack had only grown better looking over the years. He still resembled the hero of her fantasies. "How did you get in here?" She was certain she'd locked the front door.

He looked disgustingly attractive and completely at

home; not a bit like a man who was trespassing. "You're starting with the master bedroom?"

An undertone in his voice, a kind of teasing intimacy, reminded her where she was—lying full length on the biggest bed she'd ever seen, just like a woman awaiting her lover. Well, her clothing was all wrong, but he made her feel as vulnerable as though she were wearing a transparent negligee.

He shifted in the doorway, and the awareness hovering between them made her jump off the bed as though she'd been bitten.

Gathering up her materials, she did her best to sound busy and professional. "Yes, I'm starting with this, ah, room. And I need to get some things from my van."

What she needed was to get away from Jack. And stay away.

Walking toward him felt like she was moving in slow motion.

Their gazes locked.

He didn't move.

He stayed wedged in the doorway, his deep blue eyes never leaving her. The way he gazed at her had her nerve ends shivering. He'd never looked at her that way when she was sixteen and wanted nothing more than his love. Why did he have to do it now? When she was over him, and planned to stay that way.

"I have work to do, too," he said.

"Well, do it somewhere else."

He pretended to look puzzled. "This is the McNair House, isn't it?"

She stopped dead in her tracks, halfway between him and the huge bed. A horrible premonition seized her.

"Oh, no. *Oh, no.* Don't tell me *you're* the carpenter on the job?" She should have remembered Jack was no longer a college-bound quarterback.

He nodded, so relaxed he could lean casually against the doorjamb while she was humming with tension.

Suddenly, she didn't feel like a busy professional. She felt like a confused teenager. "But I've already started, so you'll have to tell the committee you've changed your mind."

"I started last week," he countered. "Check out the windowsill." He pointed at one of the windows, and there was the telltale patch of new wood, like a Band-Aid against the darker wood of the original. "And I cleared out a couple of rats' nests in that mattress you were just lying on." He stared intently at the bulging mattress for a moment. "I hope I got them all."

"But I can't work in the same house with you," she said, frantically brushing her rear.

"Why not, Laura?" His casual voice took on an intensity she didn't like.

All the reasons jumbled around in Laura's head like bingo balls. Trying to pick out just one reason was impossible. "I...I just can't, that's all."

"Look, I'm sorry I was such a jerk to you in high school. But that was a long time ago. Surely we can work together as professionals."

This was his idea of an apology? For almost ruining her life? She had no intention of discussing the past with him. Not now, not ever. "It's not personal. It's a professional decision. I only work with people I know—and trust."

His jaw had gone kind of rigid, and his eyes no longer

smiled. "I could provide references to vouch for my work."

"From your besotted female clients? I don't think so." She moved forward again, but he shifted position so he was blocking the doorway.

"This isn't about any damn professional ethics, it's about Cory. Admit it."

"Give your ego a day off, Jack. That all happened years ago."

He scratched his stomach, causing the worn chambray to whisper over his taut flesh, and an expression that could have been remorse crossed his features. "I always wanted to explain—"

"You got another girl pregnant when you were supposed to be dating me. What's to explain?"

"We weren't exactly dating—you were all of sixteen, for God's sake."

A spurt of childish anger made Laura blurt, "And Cory was all of eighteen when she jiggled her cheerleader's pom-poms in your face—along with a few other things."

She saw he was about to speak, and flapped her hand to stop him. The last thing she needed was to reopen healed wounds. "Anyway, we've all moved on since then," she said in a determined, bright voice. "How is Cory these days?"

Jack's lips thinned. "She's just fine. Doing great. She's an anchor now at some TV station in California."

"Impressive. She still gets whatever she goes after, then?" It was a low blow, but Laura got a primitive satisfaction watching the flash of anger that crossed his face. He didn't like being thought of as a sex object, but that's all he'd been to Cory Sutherland in her senior year. If she hadn't got pregnant, she would have ditched Jack along with her worn-out pom-poms on her way to the bright lights of some big city.

He was backing away, Laura noted. No longer leaning against the doorjamb, he was standing in the doorway. Soon she'd have the room to herself again. Well, he'd brought the subject up, so she had no compunction about pursuing it until he'd backed right out the front door.

"Does Cory get back to Laroche much?"

He shrugged, took another step back. "Not too often."

She felt a frown pull her eyebrows together. "But what about the baby?" She'd be quite happy if Cory anchored at the bottom of the ocean, with Jack as her co-host, but a poor little innocent baby shouldn't suffer from her parents' mistake.

Jack snorted with genuine laughter. "The baby's eleven. Her name's Sara. She's been living with me since the divorce, and she's wonderful." She heard defensiveness as well as pride in his tone.

"When does she see her mother?" Laura asked softly. Flaky mothers she knew about.

"She gets a trip to see her mom every year for her birthday."

"I hope Cory's a better anchor than a mother." No wonder he was defensive.

He was all the way out in the hallway now. "Cory's just not the maternal type."

"And you are?"

"We're doing just fine." His tone made it clear he

didn't want to discuss the subject any further, and all signs of teasing were gone from his face.

She watched him through the doorway. "I'm happy for you, Jack. But we still can't work together."

"Why not?"

She scrambled to find a reason that wouldn't make her sound as if she still cared about him. She was astonished to hear herself say, "Because my boyfriend wouldn't like it, that's why."

Jack was back through the doorway in one stride. "Oh, right. The guy you're having all that great sex with."

She stared at him defiantly, hands on hips, willing herself not to blush. "Peter gets jealous." Which was perfectly true, and another reason she'd called it off.

"Really."

"Yes. I've ordered supplies. I've started designing. You'll have to quit."

He shook his head. "Your boyfriend's *your* problem. I'm not quitting." Then, without another word, he turned away, and she listened to the clomp of his work boots fading down the hall.

She slumped back onto the floor and stared moodily at the bed.

Seemed like all the rats hadn't been cleared out, after all.

From downstairs came the unmistakable sounds of lumber being dragged in through the front door. She drummed her fingers on the pitted fir floor, torn between stomping out of this house forever and refusing to give Jack the satisfaction of making her leave the island a second time.

Why should she? She loved this place. Besides, their respective professions made it impossible for her and Jack to work in the same space. If the project wasn't under a tight deadline, she wouldn't even have started until all the carpentry was finished.

Okay. He wasn't the carpenter she would have chosen to work with, but there was no reason for them to have anything to do with each other.

She pulled herself to her feet, her decision made. She had enough ideas to put in an order with Stan and get a few supplies here in town. That would get her out of Jack's way for a while until she was used to the idea of working with him.

No problem.

When she got near the bottom of the stairs, she inhaled the tangy scent of new lumber. Jack was dragging a load of wood into the dining room, where he'd set up a temporary work station. He'd stripped down to a T-shirt and donned rough leather work gloves. He might not be a quarterback anymore, but the size of the muscles in his arms told her he did something to stay in shape.

He used to hold her in those arms while they were necking....

Unbidden, a vision rose in her mind, of herself wrapped once again in Jack's strong arms. She imagined him touching the sensitive skin of her breasts with those rough leather-gloved hands, and was shocked at the rush of heat that surged deep inside her, and the way her nipples perked to attention. His personality might be seriously flawed, but he was so gorgeous in a rugged, laid-back kind of way that just watching him had her whole body getting twitchy.

Look, but don't touch, she reminded herself sternly, continuing down the stairs.

He glanced up then, a question in his eyes.

Although it was unspoken, she decided to answer it. "No, I'm not quitting, either. I guess I just lost my head a little back there. I was forgetting that by the time I get to a room, the carpentry's all finished, so basically, we'll hardly see each other." She pasted a perky little smile on her face and issued a part warning, part promise. "Peter won't have anything to be jealous about."

She'd expected her words to elicit some kind of agreement, even just a Neanderthal grunt, so she was more than a little surprised when Jack sent her a high-wattage grin that could only be termed wolfish. "Lady, that sounds like a challenge no red-blooded man could resist."

There was so much teasing humor mixed with the testosterone in that grin that she felt her lips quiver in response. "I'm not as easy to impress as I was at sixteen, Jack."

"No guts, no glory."

WHAT WAS HE THINKING? Jack cursed his own stupidity as he watched Laura sashay out the front door without another word.

He'd thought that working together on this project would give the two of them a chance to put his screwup behind them and rekindle the friendship they'd had as kids. And here he was, trying to lure her into the kind of sexual banter that was an easy prelude to full-scale seduction.

Trouble was, when he'd agreed to do the McNair House, he'd pictured Laura as just a taller version of the kid who used to hero-worship him.

It hadn't occurred to him that she'd be sexy as hell.

He couldn't figure out why. She had the fashion sense of a scarecrow, with those sweater-stuffed overalls she kept wearing, and her hair sticking out all over the place.

Truth was, he'd never seen a woman who could look so good with so little effort. If she wore makeup, he saw no sign of it. There was certainly no indication that she ever brushed her hair. But there was no disguising the warm glowing brown of her eyes, the creamy skin that didn't need makeup, or those very kissable supermodel lips.

And if she thought those sweaters and overalls disguised her shape, she was sadly mistaken. They hinted at curves in a tantalizing way that made him want to peek at the womanly flesh hidden under all that bulky fabric.

But how was he supposed to get near her when she wouldn't even work on the same floor?

By the time she returned, several hours later, he was getting ready to leave for the night. She lumbered in the door with a ladder under one arm and an industrial-size paint pail in the other.

"Let me help you." He rushed forward.

"Uh-uh," she grunted, but by that time he'd already arm-wrestled the heavy can away from her.

She stalked ahead of him, muttering. He thought he caught the word *caveman*, but couldn't be sure.

Once they'd dumped their respective burdens in the master bedroom, she turned to him, hands on hips, a belligerent expression on her face. "I carry my own weight on this job, Jack." She paused at his smirk. "Pun intended."

"Don't forget your grandparents as good as raised me. I'd catch hell if your gran knew I'd let a woman haul a twenty-five pound bucket of paint while I stood by watching."

The stepladder creaked as she cranked it open. "Socially, I think it's fine for you to open a door or hold a chair for a woman. But this is work. No gender biases, thank you."

"Well, pardon me. I wasn't trying to bias your gender." Whatever the hell that meant.

She glanced up at him, the rigid expression gone from her mouth. "You should know me well enough to figure out I want to be treated just like any other tradesperson."

"I hardly know anything about you anymore," he protested. "I haven't seen you since you got that art school scholarship and hightailed it out of here."

"You see me every time I come home to visit Gran."

"Not if you see me first."

"I don't know what you're talking about."

"You avoid me." It stung even to say the words.

Her cheeks colored faintly. "Why would I do that?"

He moved closer. "I don't know, why would you? Unless maybe you're still mad at me for what happened."

"Jack." She walked forward until she was standing inches from him, her big brown eyes gazing directly into his. "Hear this, loud and clear. I forgive you. Dumping me for Cory was the best thing you could have done for me."

"What?" He was so used to feeling guilty about breaking her teenage heart that it was an unpleasant shock to hear he'd done her a favor.

"You made me grow up." She dropped her gaze and caught her bottom lip between her teeth.

"Stan says you avoid intimacy."

Her gaze snapped back up to meet his, a dangerous sparkle in her eyes. "Stan reads too many self-help books. I have no intimacy problems. Really."

"Prove it."

"How?" Her eyes narrowed. She'd always been a sucker for a challenge.

"Kiss me. Right here. Right now." Where had those words come from? He'd shocked himself as much as he'd obviously shocked her. Oh, but the idea held a certain appeal, he had to admit. It must have come right from the libido side of his brain and bypassed the thinking part.

"Don't be ridiculous." Her lower lip was glossy from where she'd been biting it. No wonder his libido was putting words in his mouth.

"I think Stan's right. You're scared." He was half teasing. More than half. The grown-up Laura was so intriguing and edgy, he had to push to find out where the edges got sharp.

She glared at him for one second and then, before he knew what was happening, she'd grabbed his face between her hands and yanked him forward. He opened his mouth to protest, and found it covered by her soft, sweet lips.

Okay. It wasn't exactly a sultry, sensuous kiss. Her rigid jaw bumped his chin, and he'd probably need a visit to the dentist after she'd finished crushing his teeth between her palms. But her lips were anything but rigid. They were soft and warm and infinitely kissable.

Shock turned to amazement. His cocky libido had scored, and it was gearing up with a whole lot of other ideas. He brought his arms around Laura and snugged her up tight against him, feeling the wool and denim and all the glorious curves beneath her baggy clothes.

For just a second she let him hold her, then pulled firmly away.

He stood there trying to get his breath back while she hefted the paint pail to where she wanted it, as calm as anything.

"Got any more theories you'd like to discuss?" she asked sweetly.

3

JACK'S BOOTS CRUNCHED up the gravel drive and a familiar feeling of guilt surged when he spotted the shadowy figure in the lighted window.

He entered the kitchen and watched his daughter expertly drain spaghetti into a colander in the sink. "How's my girl?" he called softly, once she'd finished.

She looked up, her face flushed from the steam, blond hair pulled off her face in one of those plastic things that reminded him of the jaws of life.

At eleven, Sara was just starting the transition from child to woman, and she promised to rival her mother for looks. All she seemed to have inherited from Jack was the eyes. Not green and round like Cory's, but blue and almond shaped.

"Hi, Daddy!" She smiled happily, and he felt the love that rose in his throat threaten to choke him.

"Smells great, Sara," he said. "But it's my turn to cook dinner."

"That's okay, Dad, you can do the dishes."

He watched her ladle spaghetti sauce onto the pasta. The table was already set; bread steamed in the basket. Sara was so grown-up, so responsible—too responsible. A girl her age should be playing house, not keeping one.

"How was your day, honey?"

She made a face. "Okay, I guess. I got an A in the biology test. I would have brought it home but Ryan Bailey stole it and threw it out the window. He got sent to the office—" she rolled her eyes "—again."

"I bet he has a crush on you."

She looked at Jack as if he was out of his mind. "Ryan Bailey? Eeoouw!" She made imaginary gagging motions with her finger down her throat.

They ate for a while in silence.

"Why would he throw my test out the window if he likes me?" she finally asked.

Jack shrugged. "It's a guy thing."

"That is *so* immature."

"I know." He thought about Laura, and the way he'd dared her to kiss him. Talk about immature. He was as bad as Ryan Bailey. His stunt had got her attention, though—and scored him one short but pretty sweet kiss. He wondered what he'd have to do to score a few more.

"How's the old house coming?" His daughter interrupted his ingenious plans.

"It's going to be a long job, but that house will look fantastic when we're done." He was certain he spoke the truth. He saw the evidence of Laura's talent every time he visited her grandmother. The old woman complained she was nothing but Laura's guinea pig, but Jack knew how much she loved the authentic restoration her granddaughter had accomplished. The Seattle paper had even done a spread about Laura, showcasing some of her restorations in the city, and he'd been blown away by her talent. He knew how much she loved the old McNair House, and was certain it would be the best thing she'd ever done. And he'd make damn sure the parts he was responsible for were just as good.

"Maybe I could come by one day after school?"

"Sure. By next week there might be something worth seeing. Laura will have started decorating some of the upstairs rooms. So, you wanna beat the old man at chess after dinner?"

She shook her head. "Sorry, I have like piles of homework."

After dinner she headed upstairs to her room and he cleaned up the dishes.

He remembered he'd put laundry in the dryer the night before, and went to fold it, but it was already neatly stacked on his bed. Guilt hit him anew. His little girl was too serious. Why wasn't she getting sent to the office with Ryan Bailey instead of getting straight A's and folding his laundry?

Not that he was complaining. He was so proud of Sara it hurt, but somewhere, deep down, he was afraid. Afraid she didn't know how to have fun. Maybe he'd been so scared she'd turn out like her mother that he'd stifled all the fun in her.

The worst part about single parenting was having no one to talk to about it all. He would have gone to Gran McMurtry—she could always talk some sense into him—but Laura was there, and she seemed to have the opposite effect.

Laura.

He didn't want to think about her. He grabbed a pair of clean shorts from the pile on the bed and swiftly changed into running gear. At the door he yelled, "I'm going for a run, honey. Be home soon."

"Okay, Daddy" came the muffled reply.

Jack let the rhythmic pounding of his feet against the road, the steady drag of breath in and the huff out, calm him. It was quiet—just the whisper of the ocean, the sound of his feet, his breathing. The night was clear and cold, the stars chips of ice in the distance. He found his rhythm and let his mind float.

Images of Laura kept intruding. He was confused by her. She was just so damned different than he remembered. Her hair was different—that was the first thing he'd noticed. As a young girl she'd always worn it long, usually in a neat braid. Now it was short and sassy, and anything but neat. In fact, *she* was sassy. Mouthy even.

And she'd sure got over that schoolgirl crush she used to have on him. Those big brown eyes that used to worship him now looked at him like he was a damn termite.

Besides, she had a boyfriend.

Jack ran harder, sprinting uphill until each breath was painful and his shirt was sweat-plastered to his chest and back.

When he got tangled up with Cory, he'd ended up losing more than just a football scholarship. He'd lost his best friend. And that was what he missed most, he realized, as he accepted how much Laura's rejection of his very presence hurt.

He could use a friend.

NEXT MORNING, Laura didn't even glance at the dusty green truck parked in front of the house, or pause inside the door. Instead, a box of supplies in her arms, she bounded straight up the stairs and into the master bed-

room. At least she planned to. As it was, she stopped
dead at the bedroom doorway.

In the middle of the room, a shapely, if dusty, jean-
clad butt seemed to grow from the floor like a mush-
room. The top part of Jack Thomas was down a hole in
her bedroom floor, while the bottom part...

Her heart started thudding double time. Her breath
caught. Whatever he was doing down there was making his back end move and strain against the worn
denim. She watched the long muscle of his flank tighten
and relax as he worked, watched the shifting of his hips.
She felt an insane desire to squeeze her hands into the
back pockets of those old jeans. The pockets would be
warm from his body heat. They'd cup her hands tight
against him.

Forcing her gaze higher didn't help. His plaid shirt
was getting dragged out of his waistband, and a trian-
gle of tawny flesh appeared just above his right hip. She
watched, mesmerized, as it grew larger. Then a wave of
irritation at her own foolishness struck her.

"Just what the hell do you think you're doing?" she
demanded, dropping the box with a thud.

It was followed almost immediately by another thud
and a cry of pain. The top half of Jack Thomas emerged
from the hole, his hand massaging the back of his head.

He winced. "And good morning to you, too."

Laura crossed her hands under her breasts and
looked down at him. "What are you doing in here?"

He grimaced as he continued rubbing the back of his
head. He stood and turned his back to her. "Do you see
any blood?"

"I will in a minute," she said through gritted teeth. "Rivers of it, if you don't answer me."

He turned back. "Dry rot," he said briefly. "Not too bad, though. I'm checking all the floors up here."

"Wonderful. So I'm going to have sawdust floating all over the place while I'm painting? That's a new paint effect I've never tried."

He looked a little sheepish. "I thought I'd finished all the carpentry on this floor, but I found a patch on the ceiling downstairs. I could see from below that the flooring up here was affected, too." He paused. "Sorry. I'll do it as quickly as I can."

It was a reasonable explanation. She should be reasonable about accepting it. In Seattle, where she had a comfortable relationship with lots of other tradespeople, she would have been more than understanding. But this was Jack and she couldn't even be in the same room with him without feeling claustrophobic. Why couldn't he just stay out of her way?

She glared at the gaping opening in the floor. She glared at him. "I'm upstairs, you're downstairs. Remember? This is *my* room. While I'm working here you can work anywhere but. Is that clear?"

"You mean I have to keep track of your movements just to do my job? That's ridiculous." He planted his feet wide and glared right back at her.

She hated how aware of him she was. How his presence seemed to shrink the room. She wished he'd tuck his damned shirt back in.

"I tell you what," she said. "I'll make it easy for you." She dug into the box at her feet and grabbed a roll of bright blue low-tack tape. She waved it under Jack's nose.

"See this? It's very hard to miss. Wherever I'm working I'll put tape across the doorway, like this." She backed up to the doorway and peeled off a long strip of blue tape. She stretched up to attach one end to one corner, and crouched to attach the other end to the opposite bottom corner. She repeated the procedure until a large blue X crossed the doorway.

"See? X marks the spot." She spoke slowly and clearly, as though he were learning impaired. "Where you see a blue X, you don't go. Jack understand?"

He brushed past her on his way out. "I understand all right." She expected him to blast through the tape like a race car hitting the finish line, but he stopped just before reaching it.

He turned back toward her and she caught a gleam in his eye. His angry voice was suddenly suspiciously cheerful. "And I think it's a great idea. I'll use yellow tape to mark off my construction areas." He smiled like one of those cartoon snakes talking to a plump and not very bright mouse.

Laura gaped. She couldn't believe he was backing down. And she knew that smile. Her own eyes narrowed.

She watched him step carefully through the doorway, bending and twisting so as not to disturb the tape. From the other side of the X he grinned back at her, the snake about to strike. "Don't fall down any holes, now."

Too late she realized the mess he'd left her in. "Oh, no, you don't, you get back here and fix this hole...Jack!" She yelled down the hall, but the only answer was the retreating thump of his boots.

She stomped back to the hole, bent and put her own head into the blackness. "Well, if that's the way you want to play it, fine!" she yelled. Her voice echoed in the stuffy darkness along with Jack's mocking laughter.

She picked up her roll of blue tape and climbed back out the doorway, then went round to each doorway on the upper level and taped a big blue X on each one. Just for good measure, she taped a blue X at the top of the stairs.

Satisfied, she returned to the master bedroom, placed boxes around the hole and hoped to heaven she didn't trip over one of them and fall into Jack's excavation.

Safe for the moment from the marauding carpenter, she got to work. Jack could just wait until she was done and all the paint dry before he finished the floor.

She didn't emerge from the bedroom until hunger pangs urged her to climb through the blue X and seek some lunch.

Halfway down the main stairway, she stopped. At the foot of the stairwell was a floor-to-ceiling X in bright yellow tape with the words *Caution, construction site* printed over and over in black.

"Ooh." She spluttered in outrage, preparing to pull down the tape, when she found herself chest-to-chest with Jack.

"Don't touch that tape," he ordered. "This is a construction zone." He patted the hard hat he was now wearing, making his head resound like a snare drum.

She narrowed her eyes. From the bottom step she was

eye-to-eye with him. "And just how do you suggest I get in and out of this house?"

He shrugged. "This was your idea."

His lips, she noted in fury, were clamped tight to keep him from laughing in her face. His eyes were so bright with suppressed amusement they were almost crying. He thought he'd won, did he? Well, she would show him she wasn't to be beaten so easily. If she had to fashion a Tarzan swing from old drop sheets just to get in and out of the place, she would.

"Fine," she snapped. Swinging round, she stomped back up the stairs, thinking furiously. There was a tree that grew under the bedroom window...

She hung out the window as far as she could, but the cherry tree that grew outside was too far away. She'd break her neck for sure if she tried to climb down. Well, she'd show Jack she could still outsmart him.

Adrenaline, and something that felt curiously like fun, coursed through her body as she sped through all of the other bedrooms, looking for a way out. None suggested itself, but she was determined not to give in.

Maybe she should shout "Fire!" and let the fire truck lift her down.

She snapped her fingers. Of course, the fire escape. She ran back to the master bedroom and through the door to the adjoining dressing room. Attached to the dressing room window frame was a rope ladder that sagged in a dusty heap on the floor. She'd noted that the old rope ladder was the only fire escape on the second floor—something that would have to be changed before the house opened to the public.

Gritting her teeth, Laura tossed the ladder out the

window and, clinging to the window frame, climbed through. The rope was ancient, but thick, and seemed sturdy enough. Mentally crossing her fingers, she crouched and grabbed the sides of the ladder.

She felt like a kid again.

The spiky feel of sisal under her palms was itchingly familiar, prickling and burning as she hung on for dear life. Her feet flailed in space before she found a solid rung and planted them on it. She remembered not to look down, concentrating instead on feeling for each step, testing her weight on it before letting go of the one above.

She was feeling awfully smug by the time she was halfway down, and paused to admire the view of Laroche harbor and her own cleverness. That's when the rung beneath her broke.

"Oh...my...gawd," she screamed, dangling helplessly. She forgot about not looking down, and nearly fainted when she glanced below, way down at the hard ground a good ten feet below her swinging feet.

Sweat prickled the hands that were clamped on the ropes. Her arms burned. She knew she'd have to loosen her death grip on the ladder in order to move, but she was terrified. She opened her mouth to scream for Jack, then clamped it shut.

With a mumbled prayer and tightly shut eyes she slowly loosened her grip and slid down, faster than she'd planned, burning her palms, until she bumped into the next rung.

It broke. She let out another shriek, certain she was about to end up a heap of broken bones.

But the third rung held, and she didn't waste any

more time on the view, but scrambled down with her heart jammed in her throat.

The rope ladder ended while her feet were still three feet short of the lawn. Trying to keep her knees relaxed, just the way Jack had taught her all those years ago, Laura swung out, closed her eyes and dropped into space.

Two warm and solid hands grabbed her as she hit the ground, steadying her on her feet.

She spun round and stared up into Jack's face. There were worry creases on his forehead, but the crinkles around his eyes were deep with amusement, and she read admiration in the blue eyes. For a second he was the old Jack, her childhood hero, and she was proud she had outwitted him.

His strong hands spread warmth into her upper arms where they touched her. He had caught her before she hurt herself, just as he used to. She started to smile back, lost in the blue of those laughing eyes and the old camaraderie. The scent of spring was in the air, along with the tangy hint of ocean and the nearer scent of Jack. She felt an urge to lean into the strong chest and wrap her arms around him. Reach up and plant her lips on his neck.

Then reality struck. She pulled away, but he grabbed her hands and turned them over, to run callused fingertips across the burning flesh of her palms. "Better put some cream on these," he said.

She started to pull her hands back, and at the same moment noticed they weren't alone.

The Save the McNair Committee chairwoman's puzzled face appeared at Jack's shoulder. "Is there something wrong with the door, dear?" Mrs. Walters asked Laura.

"Yes, Laura," Jack echoed innocently, his eyes wickedly taunting her. "Tell us why you came down the fire escape."

Her eyes murdered him, before she turned her own innocent face to the older woman. "I just wanted to make sure, in case there was an emergency—for instance, if a deranged lunatic suddenly appeared downstairs—that I'd have another way out of the house."

"Well, that's very sensible, dear, although I'm sure Jack here could deal with any deranged lunatic callers. If we had any, which, of course, we don't. The nearest asylum is some distance, I believe."

Mrs. Walters looked from Jack to Laura and back again. "Anyway, I just came by to tell you that we're having a special meeting of the committee next Wednesday night and we'd like both of you to come and give a short progress report."

"Of course," Laura said.

"We'd be happy to," Jack agreed.

The chairwoman kept smiling at them, and only then did Laura realize Jack still held her hands. She jerked them away.

"Perhaps we'll find out who the mystery philanthropist is," Mrs. Walters said.

"Mystery philanthropist?"

"Didn't Jack tell you?"

"No." He hadn't thought she'd be interested in the little fact that they'd be working together. She wasn't a bit surprised he hadn't discussed the project's financing with her.

"The house would have been bulldozed by now, in spite of all our efforts to preserve it, if it hadn't been for a secret benefactor."

Laura had to hold back her smile; the woman was clearly agog with the excitement of her small mystery. "Really?" she said, seeing something was required.

"Oh, yes. Well, you know what the costs are like, restoring a home like this. We tried bingos and bazaars, bake sales and—" she shook her head disapprovingly "—even a casino night, but we couldn't raise the kind of money we needed. Not in time to save the house."

She shook her head sadly and her tight gray curls wobbled. "I tell you, dear, those were dark days for the committee. Then, out of the blue, the mayor came to one of our meetings and announced the McNair home had a benefactor, who wished to remain anonymous. This mysterious person is putting up half the money for the restoration.

"Of course, we're all dying to know who it can be, but it's very hush-hush. Even your grandmother doesn't know, and she always knows who's doing what in this town before they've made up their mind to do it."

Laura tipped her face to the spring sunshine. Neighborly gossip, the smell of the sea and the McNair House were all as much a part of her heritage as her brown hair and eyes. It felt good to be back.

"Well, I must be going. See you both next week." Mrs. Walters walked briskly away.

Laura glanced at Jack and found him grinning down at her in a way that made more than her palms tingle.

"How 'bout a truce?" he said.

"Why?"

"'Cause if you break your neck climbing back in that window, you'll slow the project. I'm on a tight schedule."

She grinned back at him. "Chicken. It's only because you have a child to support that I'm going easy on you. Remember that, Jack."

JACK'S ALARM JERKED HIM out of sleep. He stared blearily at the clock and groaned, before dragging himself out of bed to shut it off. It was 5:00 a.m. and he must be certifiable.

On his way out through the kitchen he glanced longingly at the coffeepot, but didn't have time if he wanted to be back again in time to eat breakfast with Sara. Quietly, he let himself out of the house and walked the few blocks to the McNair place.

He picked up the tools and lumber he needed and negotiated his way upstairs through the tangle of colored tape until he was in the master bedroom. Laura had added a new blue cross, he noted, at the doorway to the third floor. He grinned in the dim light.

She hadn't changed much from the feisty girl who never turned down a dare, climbed every tree he did and probably risked her life on several occasions pretending she wasn't scared. He'd put her in danger again yesterday, and he'd worried all day that she might fall into that damned hole.

He flicked on the lights, moved the boxes away and set to work on the floorboards with the craftsmanship he had spent years learning. When he was finished, it would be almost impossible to tell the floor had been patched.

He could see this room coming alive under Laura's talented hands, and he felt at peace working in the same room where she had worked yesterday and would work again today. He wished he could patch the hole he'd made in her heart as easily.

She'd never married. Gran didn't tell him anything about her boyfriends, and he didn't ask. He wondered who this Peter was. Did Gran know about him?

Jack should have known. He should have been a part of her life in the years since she'd grown up and moved away. He wondered how everything had got so mixed up.

She'd just been this great kid, the little sister he never had. She'd worshipped the ground he trod on, and he'd let her tag along.

Then one day, they were in the orchard of this very house. He was nineteen, so she would have been sixteen. He was a big shot then, out of school, working as a carpenter's laborer to earn extra money for college, a football scholarship in his back pocket. Oh, he'd had the world by the tail.

She'd been looking up at him, adoration in her eyes, as usual, and it was a powerful aphrodisiac. Suddenly, and for the first time, he'd seen the budding woman. Without thinking what he was doing, he'd leaned forward and kissed her.

At first her whole body, including her lips, had been rigid with shock. Then she'd melted against him, and he'd discovered there was a woman's body underneath the jeans and baggy shirt, a woman's passion just waiting to be explored.

She didn't have much kissing experience, but what

she lacked in technique she made up for in enthusiasm. Pretty soon, necking with Laura got to be a regular occurrence, and she got to be pretty good at it.

Looking back on his teenage years in this small town, where he knew everybody and their grandparents, he remembered being one pulsing hormone, constantly aroused, constantly frustrated. He'd had no business messing around with Laura. She was too young and he knew it.

One rainy afternoon, they'd been necking in the basement when his parents were out, and she'd looked up at him all vague and starry-eyed. "I love you," she said.

"Whoa, slow down" was his great comeback line. He was panting; so was she.

"I do. I love you. I want to...you know, I want to do it." Her face was crimson....

"Ouch, damn it!" Jack yelled. He'd been so busy reliving the past he'd gone and hammered his own thumb. He often wondered what would have happened if they had "done it" that day. Probably the course of history would have changed. But an odd chivalry had always possessed him where Laura was concerned.

He'd kissed her gently and said, "Not yet, Laura. Wait till you're older, when you're sure."

There were tears in her eyes when he'd pulled away. "I am sure. I love you. I'll always love you."

"I'll wait for you," he'd promised. And at the time he'd meant it.

NO GREEN TRUCK LURKED outside the house when Laura arrived, which meant one less encounter with Jack. She relaxed her shoulders and walked through the front door, a portable stereo in one hand. She noted he'd removed the big yellow X in front of the stairway.

It was as she trod across the floor of the master bedroom to plug in her stereo that she noticed the neat patch where yesterday a hole had gaped. With a soft gasp of surprise, she dropped to her knees and ran her fingers over the hairline join.

She didn't know when he had sneaked back to fix the floor, but she knew she was looking at several hours worth of work. Her top teeth sank into her bottom lip while she took in Jack's message. *Let's let bygones be bygones*, he was saying, as clearly as if he'd sent a printed greeting card.

Maybe I'm not ready yet.

Soon she was perched on her stepladder, classical music playing in the background as she began the laborious job of stenciling a whimsical border of cabbage roses on twining green stems.

The stenciling brushes scrunched against the walls as she worked her slow and tedious way around the room, letting the soft strains of Vivaldi ease her boredom, while she tried not to feel warm and gushy that Jack had fixed the floor overnight.

He'd probably done it for his own satisfaction, or maybe even just to annoy her, she reasoned—but the warm and gushy feeling persisted.

Temporarily.

Before long she heard the banging and bonking that signaled she was no longer alone in the house. Then the hammering began. She turned her stereo up.

Suddenly, the sound of loud rock music entered her space like a bad smell.

Jumping down with a thump, Laura turned the Vivaldi up, way up.

Within minutes Vivaldi and Bruce Springsteen were performing an unlikely duet at full blast. Upstairs it was the *Four Seasons* in Italy, downstairs it was unquestionably the U.S.A.

Then an electric saw added to the cacophony; Laura's brush jerked, jabbing pink all over where a green stem should be. She opened her mouth to scream in frustration when there was sudden silence—and all the lights went out.

The house had taken part in the quarrel and blown a breaker.

Ashamed, she jumped down and pulled the plug on her stereo.

After the lights came on, only the noise of the saw floated upstairs.

4

"WANT SOME COFFEE?"

Laura jumped at the sound of Jack's voice.

He stood outside the bedroom door, two ceramic coffee mugs and a stainless steel thermos thrust through the doorway—and a hopeful expression on his face.

"Peace offering?" She glanced down from the top of her stepladder. The very idea of coffee made her salivate, and her neck was literally aching for a break.

"Yeah, I guess. We never did like the same music." He followed the coffee stuff into the room.

She paused, knowing it was a bad idea to get too close to Jack. But right in the middle of the floor was that new patch of flooring...and besides, the coffee smelled *so* good.

"I'd love some. Just let me finish this bit."

Behind her she heard the clink of metal on ceramic, the hiss of pouring coffee and then nothing. She had the idea Jack was watching her.

Determined to act casual and friendly, which she supposed were terms of the truce, she asked a question she'd been wondering about. "How come Laroche suddenly wants this house fixed up, after all these years?"

"A developer put in a bid to buy the property. He plans to knock down the house and build condos."

Her stenciling arm stalled and she turn to stare at Jack. "Condos?"

He chuckled. "From the sound of disgust in your voice I'd say you don't approve."

"Of course not. Do you?"

He shrugged. "It's progress, Laura. It might bring some new people into Laroche, and that would help the economy."

"Oh, come on. You love this house as much as I do. Remember when we used to sneak up here?" He'd loosened a few of the boards nailed over the windows, so he could pull them aside and they could peer into the dusty depths of the empty ground-floor rooms. It would have been easy to sneak right into the house, but, by unspoken agreement, they never had.

"Why do you love it so much?" Jack had asked her once when they were standing side by side peering in the window.

She'd turned to him in surprise. "Can't you feel it? There's happiness in this house. It's a house built by love."

He'd snorted in adolescent male superiority. "Love? It was built with first growth timber, that's what's great about it. Your grandpa told me the beams in the house are real trees, some with the bark still on 'em. And the wainscoting in the dining room is in four-foot-wide panels—can you imagine trees so big you could cut four-foot panels out of them?"

Laura hardly listened. She was dreaming, bringing the past and the future together in her fantasy. She heard Jack say in his cocky way, "This place'll be mine someday."

Ours, she'd promised silently. The rooms were empty and sad, bereft of the family that had made the house a home. But Laura's imagination painted all the rich colors of life back into those rooms.

"I guess that was the first time I thought about interior design as a career," she said aloud.

"That was a long time ago." He sounded almost sad. Maybe he missed their early friendship as much as she did.

"Yeah. But it's kind of amazing that we both ended up working on the house." She scrubbed and swirled the paint along the rest of the wall and into the corner where two walls met. A good place to stop. She climbed down the ladder, letting her neck roll.

Jack relaxed on the floor, long legs stretched out, his back propped against the wall. He held a steaming mug up and she took it gratefully, squatting down beside him.

Okay, a truce. I can do this. "So how's the downstairs coming?" she asked.

"The stenciling looks great," he said at the same moment. They stopped.

He looked at her, his eyes crinkling. She felt her own eyes twinkling back.

"If you want to put your classical music back on, it's okay with me." He leaned over her to switch on her ghetto blaster, his arm brushing hers in a light, warm touch. Vivaldi's musical "Spring" blossomed in the room.

She cradled the mug, trying to pretend the warmth flooding her came from the coffee and not Jack's casual touch. Her coffee mug was bright yellow and advertised a building supply company. Jack's mug was a faded red. A picture of a prize ribbon announced #1 DAD. She smiled.

Jack's eyes followed hers. "Sara gave that to me for Father's Day a couple of years ago."

"She must love you very much."

"It's not like there's a lot of competition for her affection." He said it quickly, bitterly. As Laura looked at him, surprised, he seemed to collect himself. "But we do all right."

"It must be tough being a single parent." It was hard to think of Jack as a father. Laura rubbed her sore neck absently, in her mind's eye seeing the young Jack racing down the school playing field, football clutched under his arm. This was how she always pictured him. "Do you regret giving up the football scholarship?"

"Only every day of my life." He turned to her suddenly, his eyes intense. "You don't know what it's like. You got out of this little town. Almost everybody we knew got out. Even Cory cut out after five years. Everybody except me." He looked away, frowning.

"But Jack...I always thought you loved it here."

"I do, but that doesn't mean I want to stay in a place where everybody knows your name and what vegetables you like and checks your laundry line so they know your favorite brand of underpants."

Laura laughed. "It can't be that bad."

"Trust me. I'm the one who does the washing and buys the underpants. While other guys worry about what shirt to wear to a meeting, I'm trying to figure out what to buy for dinner, checking homework, getting the dishes done so we have something to eat off at night and still trying to get to work on time. There ought to be a union."

"Why, Jack, you're a feminist."

He couldn't have looked more shocked. "I am not!"

"Sure you are. You gave up your chosen career to look after your child, and you resent the lost opportunities. You've picked up every woman's burden. Kids, housework, dishes and a job. Now you know what women have been complaining about for years. Maybe you should burn some of those underpants in protest."

He looked down his nose disdainfully. "And what do you know about it?"

"Enough to stay single."

He shrugged.

She felt his pain and wanted to reach out in some small way and help him, amazed at how easily they seemed to pick up the threads of their old friendship. "Jack, couldn't you take Sara with you if you want to leave town?"

"And take her away from her friends? Her home? You of all people should understand how important that stability was for her when she felt abandoned by her mom."

Laura felt stupid not to have seen that. Her own mother had been totally caught up in the hippie era. Especially the free love part. Laura knew she'd been conceived in the back of a van on a moonlit night, and that, consequently, the boy who was her father wanted to name her Moonbeam. Gran had naturally put a stop to that. She'd even made the hippie parents get married. Then she and Grandpa had brought Laura up, while her mother dropped in from time to time. A lovable and exuberant houseguest, but nobody's idea of a mother.

Laura wondered if Sara missed having a regular mother as much as she had. It was still tough to imagine a real girl, Sara, when she thought of the baby. A baby growing up with a single dad who never got his chance at glory. "I'm sorry, Jack."

He looked even more uncomfortable. "You make a mistake, you take responsibility for it." He looked down at the mug. "What am I saying? She's not a mistake, she's the best thing that ever happened."

Laura nodded. "She just came too soon," she said softly.

He took a sip of the steaming brew. "Yeah," he murmured.

She thought for a moment. "You know, one of the things we feminists agree on is that both parents have to take responsibility for kids."

His head shot around and the scent of citrus shampoo wafted into the air. "One of the things Cory and I agreed on when we got divorced was that Sara stay put. This is her home. And until she's eighteen it's my home, too. That's it. I'm not having her trail around half the year from TV studio to TV studio after her mother."

They both drank coffee silently for a while. Laura knew when she'd hit a brick wall, and Jack's tone was solid brick. Then he touched the hand that was still rubbing her neck, making her jump. "Turn around," he ordered.

"It's nothing, just a cramped muscle."

"It'll get worse if you ignore it."

She tried to turn her head to glare at him, and yelped.

"Trust me, I can fix it." He waved his hands like a magician in front of her. "I'm the handyman, remember?"

Deciding it was easier to give in than to argue, Laura turned her back to him. His long fingers settled on either side of her neck, not rubbing, just touching, pressing their way down until he connected with a lump of pain and she grunted.

His fingers were firm and soothing as they kneaded her muscles, starting just under her jaw and working slowly down. By the time he slipped his hands under her bulky sweater and moved onto the naked flesh of her shoulders, she was beyond protest. She could feel the corded muscles in her shoulders loosening under the magic of Jack's hands. She tried to think only of those hands and ignore everything they were connected to, but it was impossible. There was a warm space behind her, heated by his body. She heard his breathing, even felt it, soft on the back of her neck. He felt so good, so warm and solid. If she just leaned back into that warmth...

She jerked upright, rigid. What was she thinking?

"Did I hit a tender spot?" His voice rumbled behind her.

"No, no. It feels much better, thanks." She heard the false brightness in her voice. "I better get back to work now."

She jerked to her feet and he followed suit, raising his arms over his head.

"If you do some stretching before you start, and at the end of the day, it should help stop the muscle spasms. And remember, there's a doctor in the house."

"Who'd better check the health of the rest of the bedrooms up here. I'll be finished this one by the end of the week." She turned and wagged a finger at him. "I find your butt sticking out of another room I'm working on and I'll use it to score a field goal."

"Overworked and underpaid," he grumbled on his way out. She heard the smile in his voice, felt the answering tug of her own lips.

Laura was halfway up the ladder when he popped his head back in. "I have to go downtown this afternoon to look at another job. Anything you need done that can't wait till tomorrow?"

"I don't think so, I'll just be finishing..." Her gaze landed on the gigantic bed pushed against one wall. She climbed back down the ladder. "Oh, there is one thing. Can you help me move the bed away from the wall?"

"Oh, no, you don't. You and your neck will not move heavy furniture for a while." Even as her lips formed a protest he shook his head. "Doctor's orders. I'll get a buddy to help me move it before I go."

"That's ridiculous. I'm no wilting flower, Jack." She took a step toward the bed.

He moved in front of her and glared. "This has nothing to do with gender bias. If you end up flat on your back and can't finish the job, the house won't be ready in time. That's bad for my reputation. And I have to make my living in this place where everybody knows everybody's business. Got it? I'm not being chivalrous, I'm looking out for my own interests. Moving furniture is on *my* list."

"Well, make sure it's moved before I get to that wall."

He left without another word.

She stalked after him. "You were never this domineering when we were kids."

He turned, looking down the bridge of his nose at her. "You were never this much of a pain in the—"

"Ja-ack, you in there?" a hearty male voice boomed from below.

"Up here," Jack shouted back.

Footsteps pounded up the stairs then a dark head emerged into the upstairs hallway. "Hiya, Jacko!"

"Hey, Chipper!" The two locked hands in some weird, twisted handshake. "I didn't know you were in town."

"Just here for a few days, to start getting the place ready for summer." If ever a nickname suited anyone, Chipper's did. He was the bounciest person Laura had ever seen. He was never still, and his round girth only added to the bouncy-ball look of him.

"You remember Laura Kinkaide, don't you?" Jack said, gesturing to her.

"Laura? You mean from high school? Wow, you turned out gorgeous."

She grimaced. "Only when I've got paint in my hair."

She found herself enveloped in a bear hug. "Hi, Chip," she gasped weakly, when she could breathe once more.

"Great to see you again. Oh, this is great. I came by to ask Jack to a barbecue. First of the season—at my little summer place, on Saturday. Now you can both come."

"Oh, no, I, uh…can't," Laura sputtered. The last thing she wanted was a high-school reunion.

"Don't tell me you got a hot date, because all the decent guys are coming to my place. Honest. It'll be like old times."

Exactly what she was afraid of. "But I can't leave Gran—"

"No problem, bring her. Jack can pick you up so you don't have to worry about finding my place." His round eyes twinkled with excitement. "Oh, this is going to be great!" he repeated.

He was rolling back toward the stairs, beaming.

"But, Chip," Laura began, trying again.

"Yeah, Chip. We've got a little job for you before you run off. A bed to move. In here."

While the men heaved and grunted, wrestling the bed away from the wall, Laura tried to work out a graceful way to refuse Chip's invitation.

She had a feeling he was going to shove all her objections aside, and decided the best course of action was the most cowardly: a brief but violent illness she'd just scheduled for the weekend.

"So, we'll see you both Saturday, then?" Chip puffed, mopping his wet forehead with the back of his hand.

"You bet," Jack said.

"I'm looking forward to it," Laura lied.

She caught Jack's look of surprise and smiled her most innocent smile.

THE HOUSE FELT VERY EMPTY all afternoon without the buzz of the saw, the sounds of activity, Jack's occasional whistling. Vivaldi gave way to Chopin and then silence. Laura began to hate the sight of cabbage roses as the afternoon wore on. Her neck was getting worse, but there was no way she was giving up until she had every last rose banged into the wall.

She'd paused to rub her neck when she suddenly had the eerie sensation that she was being watched. Feeling a bit goose bumpy, Laura tried to remember if there were any ghosts associated with the McNair House. She was scoffing at her own silliness, refusing to turn around and scan an empty room, when she heard footsteps approaching.

Laura turned quickly, and there was Cory Sutherland standing in the room, looking even younger and prettier than she remembered. Laura had aged twelve years since she'd last seen Cory. No way could the other woman have gotten younger, even working in TV. Laura did what any sensible woman would when confronted with a horrible apparition.

She screamed.

The apparition jumped about a mile and scuttled back against the wall. For a moment the two stared at each other, mirroring terror. Laura climbed down the ladder on trembling legs.

"C-Cory?" Laura's voice came out thin and ragged.

"I...I was looking for my dad." The young girl's voice wavered.

"I thought he was d-dead." God, yes, Mr. Sutherland had died before Cory ever came to Laroche. Maybe she'd come back to haunt Laura. But didn't you have to be dead to haunt someone? Maybe Cory *was* dead, and had taken a wrong turn to the great beyond, looking for her father. The stencil brush was so wet with sweat it slipped out of Laura's shaking hand and landed with a plop on the fir floor.

"Dead!" the voice shrieked in disbelief. "But I saw him here this morning...downstairs, through the window."

Oh, God. Laura had to get out of this spook house and fast. "Mr. Sutherland was downstairs? This morning?" She flattened herself against the wall just to stay upright.

"No, my Dad!" The ghost was near hysteria. "Jack Thomas."

Not even the wall could hold Laura up anymore. She sank to her haunches as the world righted itself once again, and she realized it was Cory's daughter staring at her like she was a lunatic, not Cory herself.

"Oh, my God, I'm sorry. Jack's fine, he just went to do an estimate on another place. I just...uh, hang on a minute, I have to stick my head between my knees." Laura gulped air until the wood grain of the floor stopped acting like a kaleidoscope and the roaring in her head slowed to a mild rumble. She raised her head cautiously. The girl was still there, looking equally cautious.

"You must be Sara," Laura said finally.

"Yeah!" The girl used the same tone as if she'd said "Duh!"

"You look a lot like your mother. I got confused."

The girl across the room was getting some color back in her cheeks. "You thought I was my mother? But why would my mother be looking for her father? He's dead."

"I know."

"Did you think I came here looking for a ghost?"

"Yes."

"Oh." The girl snickered. She tried to squelch it and it turned into a snort. Which made her giggle.

"If it makes you feel any better, I thought *you* were a ghost, too." Laura's own voice was wavering. There was a sound like the air being let out of a balloon. Laura wasn't sure which one of them made it, but it started them off and it was a long time before they could stop laughing.

"By the way, I'm Laura Kinkaide." The statement for some reason turned out to be the punch line of the joke, and they started laughing all over again.

Laura's sides were aching and her cheeks wet with tears when she finally slumped against the wall, spent. "You look a lot like your mother."

"Dad thinks she's pretty," the girl said wistfully, and then her cheeks flamed. "Oh, I didn't mean..." She had a sweetness to her that Cory never had. And when Laura looked into her stricken eyes, they weren't Cory's eyes at all, but Jack's. If she'd thought about it, she would have dreaded meeting this child—the living evidence of Jack's betrayal. But this wasn't some abstract baby, staring at her with Jack's eyes, it was a shy and vulnerable young girl.

"She is pretty. But you're prettier."

Sara looked shocked, wanting to believe and not daring. That incredible insecurity struck a chord in Laura. She remembered feeling just like that. So sure she was gawky and unattractive that she treated praise like charity.

"Is it all right if I hang around till my dad gets back?"

Laura felt the child's loneliness as an echo of her own.

"Anybody who hangs around here gets a job. I could

sure use some help with this stenciling. And besides, you owe me for scaring the life out of me."

"But I don't know how—"

"If you can hold a pencil, know how to climb a ladder and can see, you have all the skills required."

The girl stepped forward hesitantly, tucking the long blond hair behind her ears in a nervous gesture. "But you're, like, famous. My dad showed me a newspaper article with pictures of you and some of the old houses you fixed up. I couldn't..."

They'd done that feature more than a year ago. Laura had had no idea Jack had even seen it, and here he'd kept it all this time, even shown his daughter. A rush of pleasure mixed with pride skittered in her stomach. Her smile was even brighter as she assured Sara, "Sure, you can. There's nothing to it. And if you make a mistake, you paint over it. Big deal."

"Okay. That'd be awesome."

Laura eyed the girl's ragged jeans and oversize shirt apprehensively. "I have an extra smock if you need one...."

Sara was looking at her like she was crazy again. "These are my old ripped jeans."

"Well, I thought maybe some designer ripped them and they cost hundreds of dollars."

Sara looked Laura up and down, taking in the paint-stained T-shirt and overalls. It was pretty clear what she thought of Laura's fashion sense.

"Okay, here's how to find the register so you match the stencil exactly."

The blond head was bent, concentrating on every word, as Laura showed her what to do, and in minutes they were working together, Sara on the ladder and Laura perched on a stool she'd dragged up from downstairs.

Jack's daughter was shy at first, hesitant to make a mistake, and so Laura's conversational lures sank like rocks. But once Sara got the hang of it, she seemed to lose her shyness, and soon they were chatting like old friends.

"What subject do you like best?" Laura asked.

"I don't know. Science, I guess...except, last week, this boy threw my test out the window."

"He probably likes you."

"That's what Dad said. But I don't get why a guy would throw your test out the window if he likes you."

"Honey, if you ever figure out how a man's mind works, let me know."

"SO I'M CRUISING DOWN the highway with the top down, you know, gettin' the old 'vette ready for summer—" Chip mimed his actions, chubby hands moving up and down with the imaginary steering wheel "—and this megababe drives by and gives me the look. She turned her head and watched me drive past— I mean, she had love in her eye."

"Another Corvette fan?" Jack asked. The town's only pub was filling up. He kept lifting his frosty beer mug in salute to some acquaintance or other. He wished for a moment they were in some hole-in-the-wall bar in New York, where nine million people didn't know him.

"Ouch, what's got into you?" Chip asked. He leaned forward to answer his own question. "Woman trouble."

"I stay away from women. It keeps me out of trouble."

"Oh, ho. Sounds to me like the oil needs changing there, buddy. A tune-up and some body work also required." Chip winked broadly. "Tell you what, next time you get to Seattle, I know some nice ladies you could call. I mean *nice*."

Jack couldn't think of anything worse. "Thanks, Chip, but my oil's fine. If you know what I mean." He winked back. He hadn't "had his oil changed" since Laroche's only pharmacy had switched hands. Sonja, the divorced pharmacist, who liked things as discreet and uncomplicated as Jack did, had moved away soon after the new owners took over. That was almost two years ago, but Chip didn't need to know that.

Jack took a long, cool drink of beer.

"So how are things with Laura?"

"Fine." He said it in a tone meant to ward off further inquiry.

"I remember she used to have a real crush on you," Chip reminisced. He was never one to catch a subtle hint.

"I think she got over it." *And how.*

Chip leaned forward. "You blow a little on an old flame, it might get real hot. You don't know until you blow."

"I don't think so. Anyway, she's G.U."

Chip snorted at their old code. "Geographically unsuitable is when she goes back to Seattle. In the meantime she's right under the same roof. It doesn't get any better."

Except that after the job, she'd go back to Seattle and

Jack would still be here, stuck permanently in Laroche by the Sea.

Chip put on a knowing air. "She's a painter. Check out her technique with edible body paint."

Jack choked and spluttered. "What?"

"Oh, it's great! Comes in different flavors and colors...banana yellow is a personal favorite." He leered. "With Laura and you working together all alone in that big house, interior decorating takes on a whole new meaning."

Jack was ready to stick something, like his fist, in Chip's grinning face. "We work together. That's all."

Something of his thoughts must have come through in his tone, for Chip backed away. "No offense, buddy. It was just a joke. And if I was spending eight hours a day in a deserted house with Laura I'd—"

"Well, you're not," Jack snapped. "I gotta go."

"See you Saturday!" Chip called after him, unfazed, as Jack shouldered his way to the door.

After the noise and warmth of the pub, the street outside seemed quiet and cold. Jack started to head home, then changed his mind and walked back up to the McNair House. The lights were still on upstairs. He checked his watch: 5:15.

Even though their contracts were separate, he didn't want Laura to think he was a slouch. He let himself into the house, and was surprised to hear female voices upstairs. Curious, he mounted the stairs swiftly. As he moved down the hall to the bedroom, he distinguished Laura's voice and was sure the second voice belonged to Sara.

Except she sounded so lively. He slowed his steps and approached the doorway silently.

They were both in there, chattering like old friends. Sara had a pencil and ruler and was measuring a few feet ahead of Laura and her stencil brush. They weren't talking about anything much. It sounded like Sara was telling Laura a story about something that had happened at school. But it was a Sara he wasn't used to. It was a relaxed, giggling girl. And Laura, who had every reason to hate the sight of Sara, was listening with interest, her full lips quirked in a smile.

As Jack watched them from the doorway, unobserved, he felt a weird shifting somewhere in his chest. He tried to slip away as quietly as he'd come, but perhaps he made some slight noise, for even as he backed out of the room, Laura turned. Their eyes caught and held while Sara prattled on.

Laura's full lips parted slightly—lips as soft and pink as those foolish roses she was stamping all over the walls. The moment stretched while he stood transfixed under her gaze, as though she could see into his very soul, and he into hers.

Laura gave a little gasp and broke eye contact. "Your dad's here, Sara," she said, interrupting the flow of chatter.

"Dad!" Sara beamed down at him. "Laura said I could help her. Look, we're almost done. Can I stay till we're finished? Please?"

"She's been a great help," Laura added, addressing one of the painted roses as though she didn't want to look at him again.

He took a breath. "I've got a few things to finish up

downstairs. Why don't you come and get me when you've finished helping Ms. Kinkaide?''

Jack heard a little spurt of feminine laughter behind him, quickly squelched.

"Really, Jack, if it's all right with you, I prefer Laura."

Jack had a feeling she'd been "Laura" all afternoon. He shrugged. "Sure. Just don't let Sara be a nuisance."

He got himself organized for the morning, stacking lumber and measuring lengths of flooring, ready to cut. He tried not to feel jealous that Sara wanted to spend time with a complete stranger rather than with her own father.

He couldn't figure out what was going on since Laura had arrived. His quiet, dutiful daughter was suddenly giggling and chattering like a magpie. His old friend Chip, who used to be one hell of a wide receiver, was talking about edible body paint and Laura in the same breath.

Jack was the only one who seemed to keep his sanity where Laura was concerned. The whole thing was putting him in a foul mood. Unlike Sara and Laura, who looked to be in wonderful moods as they came giggling down the stairway like best friends, instead of a young girl and a virtual stranger old enough to be her mother.

"Okay," Jack said gruffly. "Let's get home so we can have dinner done and your homework finished before midnight."

His mood effectively dimmed theirs, and he had the dubious satisfaction of seeing his ebullient daughter relapse into her usual quiet self.

"Sorry, I guess I kept you too late, Sara," Laura murmured. "It sure was fun, though. Maybe...if you get permission from your dad...we can work together again sometime."

Sara beamed at Laura, who smiled back. "'Night, Sara, Jack," Laura said, and headed out the door.

Jack grunted a reply.

HE STAYED GRUMPY all through dinner. Sara escaped to her room with her homework as soon as she could, leaving Jack prey to his own thoughts. It seemed to him things had been going just fine before Laura arrived.

Now, seeing her every day, hearing her laughter and soft voice, noticing her curves—which not even the bulkiest overalls could hide—he realized how much he missed having a woman in his life. He hadn't felt this restless or lonely in a long time.

Cory hadn't been a perfect match. In fact, she and he couldn't have been worse suited, but she'd been there when he got home at night. And in the first couple of years, when Sara was small, they'd managed to fake a sort of happiness together.

But once she'd left, Sara had kept him on the straight and narrow path of virtue. He never got past the most casual relationships with women. Just the idea that Sara might wake early and find a strange woman in her father's bed was enough to douse his libido.

If Sonja hadn't worked the late shift at the pharmacy, allowing them time together in the mornings, while Sara was at school, he would have stayed celibate. As it was, the casual affair had been passionate at the beginning, friendly at the end, and they'd parted with some pleasant memories and no regrets.

He hadn't seen a woman he wanted since Sonja had left. Not until Laura came back.

It hit him then, the source of his foul mood. Hit him with a stunning sense of clarity.

He wanted Laura.

He'd wanted her when he'd rubbed her neck and had her skin, warm and creamy and feathery soft, beneath his fingers. His hands had wanted to move from her shoulders and slip down to caress her breasts—wanted it with an intensity that made him dizzy.

Then Chip had thrown the image of edible body paint into his mind, where it had taken stubborn root and begun to flower into graphic fantasy.

The bitter truth was Jack wasn't just in need of a woman. It was Laura he wanted. Laura, who lived miles away and had her own world, job and boyfriend. Laura, who had offered him everything once, only to have him throw it back in her face.

Even if he could somehow get past all that, he could only have her briefly; he could never keep her. She wouldn't move back to Laroche. And he couldn't leave. He wouldn't do that to Sara.

He groaned. Then he swiftly changed to shorts and sneakers and he ran.

Right into Laura.

She was just coming up the path to his house as he came hurtling out, ready to squash all his demons under his Nikes. She gasped and jumped back, while he tried to put the brakes on.

As collisions went, it was mild enough, but the bumping of their bodies sent the smell of her hair into the air. She looked freshly showered, and her shiny, chestnut-colored curls smelled of...almond-scented shampoo. Instinctively he caught her arms in his hands as he plowed into her.

"That's an effective security system you have," she gasped. "Remind me to phone first next time."

He laughed softly, letting her go. Abruptly his churlishness seemed to vanish. "Sorry. Did you come to see Sara? I'll tell her you're here."

With a hand on his arm, Laura stopped him going back into the house. "No. I came to talk to you." She looked him up and down. "But obviously it's not a good time. I can talk to you tomorrow at the house." She turned.

"No, wait." He was eager to hear whatever she had to say to him. "I was just going for a run. If you give me five minutes to put something warmer on, we can go for a walk instead." `

"If you're sure—"

"I'm sure."

They set out on foot from Jack's house and walked by unspoken agreement toward the waterfront park. The shush of the ocean and the occasional barking dog were the only sounds. They didn't talk much. Jack left it to Laura to open the conversation when she was ready.

She waited until they were in the park, walking on one of the narrow paths. He heard her take a deep breath, as though she were about to give him some bad news. His heart sank. Maybe she was leaving, just as he was getting reacquainted. Just as Sara seemed to have found a woman to talk to.

"Jack, I'm sorry if I was out of line today. I mean with Sara. I don't know much about kids. I guess I should have checked with you first, before I let her help me." In the dim light he saw her biting her lips. "I was thinking it might happen again, and I wanted to discuss with you—"

"I was a real pig today," Jack interrupted. "I should be the one apologizing. You didn't do anything wrong." He stopped walking, grabbed her arm and turned her to face him. "You were wonderful with Sara. She needs someone like you in her life. A woman she can talk to."

In the moonlight Laura's hair gleamed. Her lips seemed to shimmer, smiling up at him in relief, drawing him forward.

"She's lonely, she could use a friend...." His throat felt thick. He wasn't just talking about his daughter's needs anymore. Warning bells started clanging in his head, telling him to back off while he had the chance, but his lips had other ideas. He dipped his head slowly, making his intention clear, giving Laura a chance to duck away.

She didn't, just stood there staring up at him, her eyes dark pools of mystery. When their lips touched he let his eyes close and gave himself up to the sensations.

Her lips were moist, cold at first and then rapidly warming as she leaned into him. It was a chaste kiss, a cautious kiss, but Jack felt the tremors it set off right down to his toes.

She pulled away first, with a jerk and a gasp.

"I'm sorry," he rasped. He wasn't sure if he was apologizing for being a pig earlier or for kissing her now. Both, probably.

They were quiet as they walked home, even more

awkward now that the kiss was between them—a real kiss, not that mashing of lips he'd dared her into earlier.

They arrived back at his house and both hesitated.

"Coffee?" he asked, uncertain whether he wanted her to stay or go.

She paused as if equally uncertain. "No, I'd better get back."

He watched her walk away, then wished she had stayed. She turned once and they gazed at each other in the dimness. She lifted her hand in a little wave and he waved back, but he didn't go into the house.

He kept watching her until she was out of sight.

5

LAURA WRESTLED WITH a bolt of vintage navy-and-yellow brocade, trying to drape enough of it over the curtain rod above the window so she could stand back and decide whether the colors worked. But every time she stepped back the draped fabric uncoiled, like a snake whose charm has run out, and flopped to the floor.

She felt hot and annoyed, and her hair seemed to be picking up static from the heavy brocade—not to mention dust. Jack was off, again, when she needed a second pair of hands. Although his absence this morning had at least saved her from having to face him.

Her lips still tingled every time she thought of that odd kiss. She could pass it off as a friendly little peck, his way of apologizing for his behavior with her and Sara.

What she couldn't pass off was her reaction. When he'd kissed her it was like a match to dry kindling—she'd flamed at his touch. Her whole body had cried out for him, wanting to wrestle him to the ground and embarrass the watching seagulls.

It wasn't fair that he should still get to her like this, she thought in despair. But one thing was certain. She wasn't going to let him see how he affected her—or let him close enough to do it again.

She was stuffing the brocade yet again over the inadequate wooden rod when she heard a sound behind her. Remembering her foolishness over the ghosts of Cory and Mr. Sutherland, she turned, fully expecting to see Jack or his daughter.

And froze.

The brocade avalanched to her feet, unnoticed. This time the person facing Laura could only be Cory Sutherland.

And she was no ghost.

The perfect cheerleader had matured into the perfect anchorwoman. Sleek, sophisticated. She was wearing a Chanel suit in pale green, which brought out the incredible color of her eyes. Her gleaming golden hair was drawn back in a chignon. Her body still looked as perfect as when it had bounced on the football field. There was not so much as a hint in the flat abdomen and slim hips that she had carried a child.

Laura felt like some kind of science experiment with her hair frizzed out with static, her makeup-free face sticky with dust. She wasn't even wearing her best overalls. Ten years of work rebuilding her self-confidence burst like a soap bubble.

"My gosh, it's Laura Kinkaide." Surprise inflected the well-modulated voice. "I'd have known you anywhere."

And thanks for that, Laura thought. "Hi, Cory," she answered weakly, wishing in the meanest, darkest part of her being that Cory *was* a ghost who could be laid to rest, or exorcised, or something.

"I was looking for Jack. I heard he was working here?"

Laura felt herself blushing, which infuriated her. As though his ex-wife would care that they'd shared the shortest kiss ever recorded.

"He's working on the downstairs. I'm working on the upstairs." She made the differentiation so Cory wouldn't get any ideas they were doing *anything* together. "But I don't think he's here right now."

"Well, if you pass each other on the stairs, let him know I'm in town. At the Seabreeze." There was a definite glint of humor in the green eyes. "It was nice to see you again, Laura."

"You, too," Laura lied.

This little job in her hometown was starting to look a lot like the high-school reunion from hell. First Jack, then Chip, now Cory.

"House," she said aloud, glaring at the heap of stubborn brocade sulking on the floor, "you're not worth it."

She glared around the room. Through the curtainless window she caught a glimpse of tossing waves in the harbor, while nearer, frilly apple blossoms twirled like parasols in the light breeze. Inside the room, midday sunshine bathed the walls and brought out the mellow rich color in the floor.

A little thrill of excitement coursed through Laura at the realization that she was finally here, working in her dream house. She smiled in spite of the wretched curtains. "Okay, you are worth it." She sighed. "And you're right, that brocade is all wrong in here."

She gathered the heavy fabric and dragged it ignominiously behind her. As she turned to the door she groaned. Jack was there, wearing one of his smirks.

"Yes," she said belligerently, before he could start teasing, "I talk to myself. Actually, I was talking to the house. The two of us have spent so much time alone together recently we're getting kind of intimate."

She hadn't meant to sound so sharp. She was still rattled from the night before and from seeing Cory so recently.

"I'm sorry. I'll make the time up." Jack sounded contrite. Her eyes widened. "Hey, it's nothing to me what hours you work. So long as you don't get in my way."

"I was, ah, hoping to talk to you. If you're not too busy."

"Never too busy to take a break." Was he going to bring up the kiss? Ask her for a date? Her heart rate sped up. What on earth was she going to say?

Jack took the lump of brocade out of her tired arms and manhandled it into the hall.

She put a hand to her frizzed hair. "Did you see Cory on your way up here?"

"Who?" The brocade got dumped once more.

"Cory Sutherland? Your wife? Mother of your child?"

"Ex-wife," he corrected automatically. Then his eyes widened. "Cory's here? In Laroche?"

"At the Seabreeze."

Whatever Jack had been about to say to Laura was forgotten. He jerked away from her, stomping on the mistreated brocade, and pounded down the stairs. It was like history repeating itself. Cory whistled and Jack went running.

And Laura was left behind, feeling like a fool.

She marched back across the room and grabbed the

antique mirror she'd picked up for the house. In its wavy surface she inspected her reflection. And learned that wrestling old fabric was not the best occupation for the complexion. Her face was lavishly decorated with bits of fluff, dust and a single curly white feather. With the frizzed-out hair on top she looked like a well-used furniture duster.

The image of Cory, smooth, sleek and perfectly groomed, flashed in her imagination. It was enough to make a grown woman cry.

JACK BROKE the Laroche speed limit three times over as he roared down to the Seabreeze. His palms were slick on the steering wheel, his stomach a knot of tension.

For five—no six—years he'd lived with fear. The fear that one day Cory would recognize what a mistake she'd made and try and take Sara away from him.

Jack didn't know much about the law, but he knew it was rare for the father to have custody of children after a divorce. He and Cory had never made their arrangement official, just split the few assets they had and agreed Sara needed to stay in Laroche. Since then, Cory had sent money when she had it in abundance, every cent of which was in a savings account for Sara's college education, and plane tickets once a year. She'd come to Laroche two, maybe three times in the years since she'd left.

Never unannounced.

Jack tried to marshal arguments as he drove the pitifully short distance to Laroche's best hotel, but he felt like a doomed man. He could imagine her reasons for taking Sara just now, and he felt a sharp stab of fear when he contemplated them.

Sara was a preteen girl. He knew nothing about the monumental changes that were ahead of her. He had a book hidden in his closet. *Now You Are a Woman* was the ominous title. He was too chicken to give it to Sara, and too scared to read it himself.

All that female stuff was daunting enough. Sara had no older woman to turn to in a mother's place, apart from Gran McMurtry—who probably didn't know any more about how panty liners had sprouted wings than he did.

Then there was the whole dating thing. He knew too much about teenage boys to let Sara go out with one. Ever.

For a few minutes yesterday, watching Laura and Sara together, he'd indulged the fantasy that Laura could be the woman he was looking for. The woman who could help Sara find her way through the maze of womanhood. But he had to face the facts. Laura would go back to Seattle in a few weeks and Sara would still be in need of female guidance.

The Seabreeze loomed ahead of him, grim against the gray rocks and gray sea, the bright trappings of summer still in storage. Al, who'd been the desk clerk at the Seabreeze for as long as Jack could remember, sent him straight up to room 201 before he even had a chance to state his business. As if he needed to. In Laroche everyone knew all about his business.

Standing in the hallway outside room 201, Jack slowly breathed in the stale air of a summer hotel in April before knocking firmly on the door.

"Come in," the familiar voice called.

He entered the room and there she was, her hunched shoulder holding the beige telephone receiver to her beautiful blond head. Her hands were busy painting her toenails. She was wearing a white silky top that showed a lot of cleavage, bent over the way she was, and her green skirt was hiked up past her knees, showing a tanned expanse of thigh.

Cory wiggled the toes of her left foot, to dry them faster, while she painted the toes of her right foot. The smell of nail polish and that wiggling and painting routine took him back to the days of their marriage.

His stomach clenched. So did his jaw. For some reason that toenail ritual symbolized for him Cory's obsession with her appearance. That and her ambition were the two things that drove her.

He didn't care what he had to do, who he had to fight, he wasn't going to let Sara grow up with this woman who had already abandoned her once.

She waved casually at him, giving a half smile.

"No, no...it's just for the weekend," she said into the phone. "Uh-huh. You can fax them to me here. I'll know by Monday...uh-huh. Gotta go."

She capped the nail polish, then put the phone back. She was wiggling both feet now. "Surprised?" She smiled brightly.

"Poleaxed."

She laughed that million dollar laugh of hers, showing a row of perfect, gleaming white teeth. He remembered when she used to cackle like a prize hen. Her agent had taught her how to laugh so she'd sound good on TV, and now he guessed she used that laugh all the time. Her cackling days, like her Laroche days, were behind her.

Her eyes roved over him from tip to toe. "You look good, Jack. Don't I get a hello kiss?"

He didn't move. He was still trying to figure out what she was expecting on the fax machine. A court order to get Sara back? She probably had all kinds of fancy friends with influence. "Not until you tell me what you're doing here," he said levelly.

She shrugged. "I had a sudden impulse to see Sara...and you, of course."

"Why didn't you call? You always call first." He jammed his hands in his pockets.

"What's going on here, Jack?" Her voice chilled. Typical reporter, to answer a question with a question.

"Nothing's going on. I just...yeah, sure. Of course you can see her." If he didn't antagonize Cory, maybe they could work this thing out.

She relaxed back in her chair. "I was thinking we should go out for dinner tonight. The three of us."

Whatever she had up her silk sleeve, Jack wanted to know about it. But he'd lived with Cory long enough to know she would tell him in her own time, in her own way. If he had to choke through a dinner to get down to the business of saving his daughter, he'd do it. He nodded curtly.

"Mmm. I'm just dying for fresh oysters. Why don't we drive to the Captain Whidbey?"

They'd spent their brief honeymoon at the rustic inn. Was it really the oysters she was after or did she want to stir up the memories of their early, admittedly passionate, times together? Or did she even remember where she'd spent her honeymoon?

"Whatever you like," he heard himself agreeing.

"I'll reserve us a table for eight o'clock. Pick me up at seven."

Irritation sluiced through him. "Sara can't hold out that long. How about dinner at unfashionable six o'clock? We'll pick you up at five."

She smoothed her hair, and uncertainty flashed briefly in her eyes. "I don't know what I was thinking of. Sorry. I'll be ready at five."

Her unfamiliar burst of contrition softened Jack. "Sara will go crazy when she finds out you're here," he said.

He left the Seabreeze and drove straight to Sara's school to pick her up. She was delighted to see him, and still more delighted when she found out her mother was in town and they were all having dinner together.

He left her at home, pulling all the clothes out of her overflowing closet while wailing she had nothing to wear. So maybe there was one thing she had in common with her mother.

Jack then drove straight to his buddy Len's law office, where he waited, hoping to be squeezed in between appointments. He finally managed to get fifteen minutes with Len and emerged feeling more depressed and anxious than when he'd gone in.

LAURA LOCKED THE DOOR with a snap at 5:00 p.m. She hadn't really expected Jack back all afternoon, not when she'd seen him tear out of the place like a tornado in his eagerness to meet Cory.

Laura didn't care what two consenting adults did in the privacy of a hotel room. She was only angry because she and Jack were under a deadline to complete the McNair job, and she seemed to be the only one at work. It was simple professional irritation that had her hands shaking so badly she could hardly get the key into the ignition.

She drove to Gran's with excessive caution, controlling the urge to push her foot to the floor and scream her way through the sedate town.

She recognized the green truck approaching from a block away. Jack was driving, but his attention was clearly on his companions. Cory's blond head was leaning toward him, and Sara's face bobbed eagerly forward from the back seat.

Laura fought the impulse to ram his vehicle. She gripped the steering wheel and took a deep breath, forcing herself not to run the smug two-timer and the ex-cheerleader off the road. The cozy trio drove past unscathed, none of them ever realizing they had been in mortal danger. In fact, none of them had so much as glanced out the window.

When she got home, Laura found Gran with her nose in *Barron's,* tsking and cheering the fate of her favorite stocks. "How was your day, dear?" she asked, without bothering to look up.

She seemed satisfied with a grunt for a reply.

"I should really buy a freezer," she said, turning a page with age-gnarled hands.

"What do you want with a freezer when you live alone?" Laura asked, pulled from her own anger by the absurd announcement.

"It's for the frozen orange juice. The way orange juice futures are looking we should stock up. The price is going to be astronomical next year."

"I love you, Gran!" Laura announced, coming up behind her grandmother's favorite easy chair to give her a hug. Her love life might be on a downhill run that showed no signs of slowing, but she could always count on Gran to make things seem better.

The old woman patted her hand absently. "Come and have some soup. I made it this morning."

Laura sniffed the air appreciatively. "Cream of broccoli? Mmm. Does this mean broccoli futures are going up?"

When they were seated at the oak table, enjoying the soup and salad and crusty rolls, Gran said, "I hear Chip invited you to a party Saturday night."

"Who told you that?" Laura hadn't bothered telling Gran about the invitation because she had no intention of going. It looked as if she'd have to fake an illness, after all.

"Chip, of course. I ran into him in the supermarket. That young man is going places."

"He already has, Gran. He's made a gajillion dollars as a stockbroker. Now he runs his own investment firm."

Gran nodded in agreement, sipping her soup daintily. "He has a good grasp of strategy, but he's too flamboyant for my taste. I'll bet he's overexposed should a correction occur."

Laura groaned inside with embarrassment. "You didn't discuss orange juice futures with him, did you?"

Gran smiled at her, as though sensing her feelings.

"Wouldn't you like to know. He did happen to mention he's single."

"For about the twelfth time." Laura crunched open a roll and spread it with butter.

"What are you going to wear to his barbecue?"

Laura glanced up into those shrewd eyes sparkling with kindness and knew she couldn't lie to her own grandmother. "I'm not going."

"Why not?"

"I'm tired. I've worked hard all week. Besides, I want to spend time with you."

"I'm flattered." But it wasn't gratitude Laura heard in the tart tone. "You forgot to mention Cory's back."

"That has nothing to do with it." Which sounded lame even to her own ears.

"I'll tell you what we're going to do Saturday. We're going shopping. We'll buy you a new dress, have some lunch out. We can spend the whole day together. Then you'll go to that party looking like a million bucks."

"But, Gran—"

"You've been going round town looking like a farm-hand in those dreadful overalls. It's time you got your-self all dressed up and showed Laroche what a beauti-ful woman my granddaughter is."

"Beauty is a state of mind," Laura answered primly.

"And there's nothing like a new dress to encourage the best state of mind." Gran's eyes twinkled.

Laura dreaded the very idea of facing her old school friends with Cory present. It brought back too many painful memories. But Gran was right, it was time she stopped running away from the past and faced her de-mons head-on. And after the way Cory had seen her earlier, she wanted to show her she really did know how to look good when the occasion required.

"Oh, all right."

"MMM, HEAVEN," Cory cooed. Her full lips caressed the oysters as she ate them.

Jack was having trouble swallowing his steak. Each piece seemed to stick in his throat. He wished Cory would just come out and say what was on her mind; he felt like he was boxing shadows.

Sara's face was flushed with excitement as she watched her mother in wonder, as though a magical princess had suddenly descended to grant her three wishes.

Cory chatted to her easily about work and some interview she'd had with a celebrity who was Sara's age. She asked her daughter about school and her friends, and Jack noticed how carefully Sara chose her words, obviously trying to impress her mother. It saddened him to see how little they knew about each other, this mother and daughter who looked so alike.

After dinner, Jack drove in the direction of the Seabreeze, still wondering when his ex-wife was going to drop her bombshell.

Cory touched his hand softly. "Jack, I'd love to come home with you for coffee." As though sensing he was about to refuse, she added, "Sara promised to show me her bedroom, didn't you, honey?"

Jack hadn't heard any such promise, and a quick glance in the rearview mirror showed Sara's perplexed look. "Oh, yeah. Sure," she said.

At the house, he put the coffee on while Cory and

Sara went upstairs together. He was torn between wanting to let Sara spend as much time as possible with her mom and wanting to stop Cory from poisoning Sara's mind with fantasies of the grand life she could live in California.

By 9:00 p.m. he'd drunk three cups of coffee, which wasn't helping his nerves, and still Cory hadn't come down. Purposefully, he got to his feet and yelled from the bottom of the stairs, "Sara, honey. It's a school night. You can see your mom again tomorrow."

He strode back to the kitchen and poured a fourth cup of coffee. He didn't have long to wait. Soon Cory strolled in and poured herself a cup, helping herself to milk from the fridge. It gave him a peculiar sense of déjà vu.

She smiled at him as she sat down. "Seems like old times, doesn't it? Like the good times, I mean." She gave him her best smile. "It wasn't all bad."

Jack felt himself smile back. "No, it wasn't all bad."

She sipped, screwing up her face. "Your coffee was always bad."

He refused to bicker about coffee. "But you didn't come here to tell me that."

"No." Cory took a breath. She seemed to be searching for words.

Jack hardly breathed, waiting.

"Sara's such a great kid. I'm proud to be her mom," she said at last.

He nodded, while worry coiled tighter in his belly. He couldn't trust himself to say anything.

"Jack, I'm worried about Sara. She's getting to an age

where she needs a woman in her life. Someone who can explain the changes she'll be going through—"

With a cry of triumph he rose from his chair and jogged into his office, where he dug out from behind a stack of woodworking magazines his reference book for the adolescent girl.

"I'm way ahead of you," he announced, returning to the kitchen and handing the heavy book to Cory.

"Now You Are a Woman..." She read the title aloud and flipped the book open. After skimming a few pages, she raised her eyes, and he saw a disturbing twinkle in them. She began flipping pages more slowly, stopping to scan the odd paragraph. "How much of this book have you read, Jack?" she asked in a strangled voice.

"I haven't had a chance to get through the whole thing yet. But I'm ready if Sara has any questions."

Cory handed him the book. "Okay, I'm Sara. I just got my first period. I don't understand what's happening to my body. Explain."

Jack feigned indifference. "Sure, no problem." He opened the book, scanned the table of contents. "Let's see, ah, 'onset of menses,' page 489. Here we go."

He cleared his throat, skimmed down to where the important stuff seemed to start, and began reading. "There are four phases to the menstrual cycle. Postmenstrual, intermenstrual, premenstrual and menstrual." He tried not to squirm on the kitchen chair. "When the pituitary gland excretes follicle stimulating hormone..." He plunged doggedly on through litanies of hormones, complex glandular workings and the mechanics of a woman's anatomy.

The diagrams were the worst. It was more embarrassing than watching those awful light days and heavy days commercials on TV. He petered to a stop.

"Well, that should answer all her questions."

"Okay, Okay, stop laughing. So I'll get another book," he grumbled.

"Jack, it's not a book you need. It's a wife, a mother for Sara."

A horrible suspicion was forming in Jack's mind. She couldn't be thinking... Surely she didn't want to get back together with him? But then, why drag them to the same inn where they'd spent their honeymoon? Why keep on about all this family stuff?

"I did this interview, the one I was telling Sara about, with this child actress," Cory was saying. "Her mother's a busy actress, too, and they hardly ever see each other. The girl was so confused, so lost."

Cory pulled a piece of hair loose from her chignon and began twirling it round her finger. "The kid's dad looks after her career...but she doesn't have a woman to turn to...." Cory's voice started to waver. "I don't want Sara to be like that."

Jack didn't think anything could be worse than losing Sara. But getting Cory back would be a very close second in the disaster department.

They'd already failed once to be a family, when they still felt passion for each other. Now he no longer felt anything for Cory except a vague irritation for the way she'd up and left him and Sara to pursue her career. As much as he loved Sara, he'd find another way to make sure she had a decent family life. He had to nip Cory's idea in the bud. And fast.

He started gently. "I know you're feeling bad now. But it could never work with us..."

Cory's eyes widened. "What are you talking about?"

"You moving back here to be Sara's mom. What are *you* talking about?"

"Oh, no, Jack." She reached out a pale, green-tipped hand and touched his arm. "I mean, you're a terrific guy, but I'm talking about finding you a *new* wife. Someone who can be there for Sara."

He blinked, wondering if too much coffee was doing something to his brain. "A new wife?"

"I'm thirty, Jack. I've got a great career, everything I always wanted. I'm even getting married again—to a producer with grown children. He doesn't want more kids and neither do I. But I need to know that Sara's happy. I'm looking for a stand-in for me."

"A stand-in? You mean like on TV?"

She fiddled with her hair some more, an old nervous gesture. "I let you both down, I know that. I hoped you'd find someone else by now."

He just stared at her.

"I don't want to be rude, Jack, but you're going to have to lower your sights a little. I figure I can make it up to you by helping you find someone else. I'm a trained journalist, after all. I know how to ask the right questions, work with body language and other signals to get at the real answers from people. We're going to put together a criteria sheet for your new wife and Sara's mother. Her stand-in mother, I mean."

Jack felt a burning pain in his lap and jumped. His coffee cup was hanging askew in nerveless hands. "*You* want to find me a wife?"

"Well," Cory said consideringly, "you don't have to marry her. At least, not right away. Let's just say a companion, a close friend. Now, I know the pickings are pretty slim on an island this size, but we'll start here, and move outward from our target center as we have to. Chip's party Saturday night is perfect timing. Most of the single women will be there. It's a wonderful place to start."

The shock was wearing off, and along with the relief of finding out he wasn't in danger of losing Sara, Jack was beginning to see the humor in the situation. His ex-wife wanted to find him a new wife. Oh, boy.

6

"GRAN, IT'S TOO SHORT." Laura bent forward before the triple mirror, and three Lauras tugged the figure-hugging red dress in the direction of her knees, which were a long way down. As she bent, her cleavage bulged over the square neckline and six hands yanked up on the bodice, only to bring the dress back up her thighs again.

"Stand still," Gran ordered. "Now turn around."

Laura did, feeling self-conscious, and yet secretly thrilled at the way the dress did things to her figure.

"You look lovely, dear," Gran announced. "We'll take it," she told the shop clerk.

"But Gran, did you see the sticker price?" Laura hissed.

"Yes. It's my treat to you for coming back and doing the McNair job."

"But...can you afford this?"

"Don't worry, I won't have to eat cat food until after you've gone."

Once Laura held the elegant bag containing her tissue-wrapped dress, she started looking forward to the party. She was also happy the shopping trip was over. "I'm exhausted. I can't wait to get home."

"Lunch will revive you, then we'll do the hair and

makeup." At eighty-two, her grandmother had more stamina for shopping then most women half her age.

"But..." Laura spread her fingers in a helpless gesture.

Gran grabbed her hands, staring at the paint-flecked knuckles and chipped nails. She clicked her tongue. "And a manicure."

"OKAY, HERE ARE my questions. What do you think?" Cory asked.

Jack took the piece of Seabreeze stationary reluctantly and leaned back in the same kitchen chair he'd sat in the night before, when Cory had first told him her ridiculous plan. On the page were ten neatly penned questions that she planned to ask some of the women at Chip's party. A second sheet was headed "Candidates."

"I'll go to the bathroom between interviews and take notes, then transfer it all to my laptop when I get back to the hotel. We can go over our results tomorrow."

"How are you going to decide which women to interview?"

"Well, you can point out the ones you like, of course, and I'll fill in with a few candidates you might have missed. Remember, we're mostly looking for someone who'd be a good mother. You might get sidetracked by other attributes."

He read the questions, felt his eyes bug out, and read them again. "I can see you asking whether they like kids, but why do you have to ask these women about sex?"

"Now, Jack, don't be coy. We used to be married, remember? You had quite a sex drive." She gave a satisfied little smile. "That was one part of our marriage that—"

"Yeah, well, getting back to the list, you can't ask a woman you've never met how often she likes to have sex. She'll think you're coming on to her."

"Jack, relax, I'm a professional. I can find these things out in subtle ways."

He was torn between horror and unholy glee. He had a feeling this was going to be a barbecue to remember. He scanned the list of questions again. "Religion, politics, financial position. You're just going to find out all about them, aren't you?"

"And if you have any questions of your own, Jack, go ahead and add them."

"No, no, I think you've got it covered. Ah, just curious. When you've found the right woman, do I get veto power?"

She trilled that trained laugh again. "Of course you do. More important, so does Sara. I'm not trying to choose your mate for you, Jack. I just want to prove to you that there are nice women out there who could make you happy. You'll have to get over me and move on."

He should put a stop to this. If he were a better man, he would. But on the other hand, if his ex-wife wanted to make a complete fool of herself, there was no law that said he had to prevent her.

He wanted to rush over to Gran's and tell Laura. She would find the whole thing as funny as he did. He pictured the way she laughed, with her head thrown back, teeth gleaming. Her laugh was natural, the kind of laugh that made you join in. Nobody had taught her how to do that.

Now, Laura was a nice woman who could make him happy. He should tell Cory to make sure her name was on the list. He would love to hear *that* interview.

Cory was frowning at the pages now spread on the table. "I wish I had a teleprompter for tonight," she said. "I don't want to forget any of the questions."

"Or the answers."

"Oh, I've got a tape recorder for that," she said brightly, pulling out a tiny stainless steel unit. "Small but powerful. It'll get their answers, no problem."

"Well, why don't you write the questions on cardboard and I'll make a flip chart. I'll stand behind the woman's head while you interview her, and every time you nod, I'll flip to the next card."

"Very funny, Jack."

"You could write the questions on your arm, like you used to before exams in school," he suggested softly.

Her color rose but she refused to take his bait. "I'll figure something out," she said primly, heading for her rental car.

"Want me to pick you up tonight?"

"Better not. We don't want anyone to get the impression you're not single. See you at Chip's." With a wave, she was gone.

He phoned Gran McMurtry. Since Sara insisted she was too old for a baby-sitter, he usually drove her to the older woman's house if he was going out for an evening. Sara always thought she was doing a good deed. Of course, Gran had her "lonely old widow" routine down pat. As soon as the evening was arranged, Jack asked to speak to Laura.

"Yes?" The tone of her voice could have put ice chips on the equator.

"Laura? It's me, Jack."

"I know."

"I just wondered whether you need a ride to Chip's tonight. It can be tricky to find."

"Thanks." The voice thawed slightly. "But he's given me directions. See you tonight."

"Wait, I—" But she'd clicked off before he had a chance to tell her about Cory's insane ideas for the evening.

He figured he'd get another chance to see Laura when he dropped Sara off, but Gran informed him she'd already left, so he drove off by himself, full of anticipation. He was looking forward to this evening, looking forward to seeing Laura, telling her about Cory's craziness and the wonderful news that Sara was his for keeps.

Ever since they'd started having their coffee breaks together, he'd felt like he was getting his friend back. Maybe more than a friend. That kiss at the beach the other night had him thinking thoughts about Laura that were definitely warmer than friendly. She hadn't pushed him away, had even seemed to welcome the kiss. He planned to ask her out, on a real date. He'd take her somewhere classy for dinner, woo her. He just wished she hadn't rushed off to the party before he had a chance to talk to her privately.

Oh, well, he reasoned as he drove up the winding

coast road, he'd haul her off for a few private minutes as soon as he got to the barbecue.

He turned into a gravel drive and immediately heard the sounds of a party in full swing. Chip's "little summer place" could have housed a family of fourteen with room left over. Clinging precariously to a bluff, it was all windows and cedar and jutting angles. The architects had designed the place to blend in with its surroundings, but in Jack's opinion it was an insult to the natural beauty it was supposed to enhance. And Jack knew the house better than most; he'd built it.

He pulled over and parked at the end of a string of cars at the edge of the driveway. Through the windows he saw the movement and color of the well-dressed crowd. As usual, Chip had managed to jam the massive house with his eclectic collection of friends and acquaintances.

Jack suffered a pang of regret. He hadn't thought to warn Laura that Chip's idea of a casual barbecue would put Martha Stewart to shame. Jack had only seen her in jeans and overalls, so had no idea if she'd brought anything else with her. Oh, well, too late now. He'd make a point of spending time with her and introducing her to everyone he knew. She used to be shy with strangers, he remembered, as he eased out of his truck and headed for the door.

He rang the bell, but no one seemed to hear it over the noise of the party, so he opened the door and stepped inside. His eyes scanned the crowd. Writers, artists, potters and business people from the island mixed with unfamiliar faces that looked like they belonged on Wall

Street or Madison Avenue rather than Laroche by the
Sea.

All the women were dressed up, he noticed with a
pang of concern for Laura. Damn. He should have
thought to warn her. He kept looking out for a pair of
denim-clad legs. If he knew his childhood friend, she'd
be hiding behind a palm or something, feeling out of
place.

As his gaze roved the crowd, searching, it snagged on
the shapely derriere of a brunette in a tight red dress,
who seemed to be the animated center of a group of
Chip's button-down friends. Whoever she was, he'd
better make sure she ended up on Cory's list.

As he moved into the room, he ordered a beer from a
uniformed waiter. He still hadn't spotted Laura, but
when he saw Cory in the corner with one of the teachers
from Sara's school, every other thought went out of his
head. The woman was backed against the window,
looking from his angle as though she were about to
plunge into the angry sea. Two spots of color burned on
her cheeks.

Cory had her purse open and seemed to be checking
her makeup while she was talking. As he watched, the
teacher gasped and stalked away. Cory then muttered
something into her lapel. So much for subtlety.

Before his ex-wife could spot him, he ducked into a
group, wondering what to do. He'd imagined Cory
making a fool of herself, but it hadn't occurred to him
that she might also offend a lot of perfectly nice women.

Where was Laura? Maybe she'd have some ideas on
how to derail his ex.

Chip's living area was a huge open-concept design

on two levels under a cathedral ceiling. Jack stood on the highest level and scanned the crowd again, frowning. He should have insisted on driving her. Gran said she'd left ahead of him, so maybe she was lost.

"Laura, honey, you look good enough to eat." He heard Chip's voice boom across the room. *Him and his edible body paint.* Jack stormed forward to head Chip and his palette off at the pass, then realized Chip was charging toward the knockout brunette he'd noticed earlier.

Jack stood there, stunned, as she turned to greet Chip with a smile and a hug. He caught a glimpse of the woman head-on.

Laura.

Chip moved on to someone else, and she caught sight of Jack. He just stood there, his mouth dry and his eyes popping out. He'd had no idea how much Laura was hiding under those overalls. But it wasn't hiding anymore.

Her figure was soft and curvy, on full display in a tight, sexy dress that caused his breath to snag. Her firm round breasts seemed to be begging for release from the bodice, and his fingers were suddenly itching to help.

He eyed her long, shapely legs and a trim waist he could span with his two hands. But it wasn't just the shape of her that held him spellbound, it was the way she sparkled. The way her personality seemed to shine tonight.

Short and perky, her hair glowed. Her eyes glittered; her cheeks were delicately flushed. Makeup enhanced her full lips and glorious brown eyes. She'd borrowed Gran's rubies, he noted, and the antique gems glittered alluringly above the modern designer dress.

She'd slain him and she knew it. The knowledge sparkled in her eyes as she walked slowly toward him.

Jack had never felt more foolish in his life. He was like a tongue-tied teenager on his first date. He licked dry lips. He tried to think of something clever and sophisticated to say, but his mind hadn't recovered from the shock. Instead he settled for the simple truth. "You look beautiful."

She smiled, letting him see the pearlescent gleam of her teeth. "These heels are killing me."

He looked all the way down those legs and caught her in the act of stepping out of her high heels. It reduced her a couple of inches to the height he was used to. He smiled down at her.

"Cory's here," she said.

"Yeah, I know."

"You didn't arrive together." She sounded surprised.

He shrugged. "I'm surrounded by independent women."

"No hogging Laura now, Jack," Chip said at his elbow. "You get her to yourself all day up in that deserted house." He winked broadly. "Give somebody else a chance."

He pulled a serious-looking Wall Street type in spectacles forward. "Laura, this is the guy I was telling you about, Albert Ferris. He's a producer. Wouldn't she be just great to host a home decorating show? Beauty, brains, personality and talent. I'm telling you, the camera would just eat her up."

Chip hadn't made a fortune being idle. He was always putting deals together; it was his nature. Other people played golf or chess; Chip put people and money together. Sometimes successfully, sometimes not.

Laura turned a startled face Chip's way. "Well, thanks, Chip, but I don't think—"

"You just tell Albert a bit about yourself. I'm stealing Jack away, there's someone I want him to meet."

Laura sent him an S.O.S. with her eyes, but Jack was dragged away under Chip's meaty wing. He flashed her a reassuring smile, promising himself he'd get back and rescue her, just as soon as somebody rescued him.

"Here's the guy I was telling you about, Slim. Jack Thomas is the best builder on the island. He built this place and I couldn't be happier. Slim here is thinking about putting up a little summer place of his own. Told him to talk to you." With a pat on the back, Chip excused himself and left the two men to shake hands.

Slim looked miserable and dyspeptic.

"You're planning to build on Whidbey?" Jack asked politely, after a moment's silence.

"No," Slim shook his head, looking even more dejected. "The Caribbean. I have an island there."

"But wouldn't you be better to hire a builder in the Caribbean?"

Slim nodded. "I keep telling Chip when I say 'the island' I don't mean Whidbey, but..." He sighed gustily.

Jack chuckled softly. "I know. He's a great talker, not such a good listener."

Out of the corner of his eye he saw that Cory had trapped his bank manager. Happily single, she was one of the nicest women he knew. She also had a legendary temper. When Cory grilled her about her financial position, she was going to blow.

And the way Mary's jaw had just gone rigid and her toes started tapping, he didn't have a moment to lose. He decided to copy Chip's favorite move.

"Ah, Slim, there's someone here I want you to meet." He grabbed the startled man's arm and pulled him in Cory's direction. Slim glanced around as though seeking a hiding place.

"Don't worry," Jack reassured the timid man. "It's not for any kind of deal. I just thought you might like to meet a beautiful woman who's a good listener. She's a TV anchor in California."

Mary, the bank manager, was starting to simmer visibly as Jack dragged Slim over to the couch.

"Cory, I'd like you to meet Slim. He recognized you from TV and was dying to meet you."

Mary jumped up, and Jack planted the hapless Slim beside Cory, pretending not to notice her grimace as he took his bank manager by the arm. "Let me get you a drink, Mary."

"TV? Is that woman doing some kind of hidden camera show?" Mary demanded in a furious undertone.

"I don't think so."

"Well, she just asked me how I get along without sex now that I'm divorced. I...I could see this list of questions she had taped to the inside of her purse."

"You know TV people," he said, trying to soothe the woman who could foreclose on his mortgage. "She's very ambitious, wants to be the next Barbara Walters. She practices all the time trying to make people angry or, better still, to get them crying. She considers it good training for her career." Jack steered her to the portable bar Chip had rented, complete with black leather bar stools.

The woman hoisted herself onto the nearest stool.

"What'll you have, Mary?"

"A martini. Double."

"Cheers!" said the schoolteacher, swaying slightly on the stool beside Mary's. He left his bank manager deep into her martini, trading stories with the teacher, while he went back to rescue Laura.

He was beginning to feel like a lifeguard.

But when he got back to where he'd left her, Laura was gone. He glanced back to discover that Slim had also escaped. Cory had a new victim, a woman he knew only by sight, but she seemed nice enough.

Too nice to leave with Cory and her list.

Jack felt sweat begin to bead on his forehead. He had to find Laura. If he could get Cory to interview *her* then he'd have time to think up a plan to get his ex-wife out of there.

After much searching, he found Laura and Chip in the master bedroom. As if he didn't have enough to worry about with Cory, now he had to chaperon Laura, who had to choose tonight, of all nights, to show up looking so delicious. He groaned mentally. God, now Chip had *him* thinking of her in edible terms.

Jack stormed in full of belligerence, to find Laura standing in the middle of the king-size bed in her stocking feet, a red-tipped finger pointing up at the wall. "You see what I mean about the 'line of vision'?" she said over her shoulder.

"Sure do," Chip said appreciatively. His "line of vision" was nowhere near where Laura was pointing; it was centered on the line of her dress riding high on her thighs.

"Hey, Jack! We were just talking about you," Chip said, completely unabashed. "Laura's going to do some decorating for me—isn't that great?"

"Great," Jack said. His voice seriously lacked enthusiasm. Laura must have noticed, for she winked down at him, her eyes dancing with mischief. "We're thinking a Middle Eastern theme. Silk throw pillows, arches. You know, the harem look."

Chip chuckled gleefully. "What a conversation piece."

"Laura." Jack jerked his head at her so Chip couldn't see. "That producer fellow needs to iron out a few details with you. He likes the deal."

"Great, great!" Chip boomed. "Opportunity calls. We can finish up later, Laura. Maybe one evening next—"

"I think that guy needs you now, Laura."

With a wave, she grabbed her shoes and left the room with Jack.

"Were you rescuing me?" she asked in an amused tone, reaching over to pull her heels back on. The way she was bending gave him a tantalizing view of her cleavage. He was going to have to put those wooing plans into high gear.

"Come outside," he urged desperately, half dragging her out onto the patio and down some stairs to the beach.

"I'm not exactly wearing my hiking boots, Jack. What's going on?"

"I don't want to be overheard." He scanned up and

down the beach, but they were alone. He turned to Laura. "You've got to help me. Cory's going to alienate every friend I ever had."

"She's had practice," Laura reminded him.

He didn't have time to go over the past, not now. "Please. She's up there interviewing to find me a wife."

Laura shook her head and pulled her hair behind her ears. "This damn wind keeps getting in my ears. I can't hear you properly, Jack."

"I said Cory's trying to find me a new wife. Well, mostly Sara a new mother," he shouted in her ear.

"That's not wind in my ear, is it. You said Cory wants to find you a wife."

"Yes."

"That's the craziest thing I ever heard." Her hair blew softly around her face. He wished he could spend some time out here, alone with Laura, instead of having to go back into that nightmare house party. The nightmare part was mostly his own fault. He should have put a stop to it when he had the chance.

"I thought it would be funny," he admitted. "I had no idea she'd make such a fool of herself and alienate every nice woman I know. Laura, she has a list of questions taped to her purse and a hidden tape recorder." He scuffed his foot against a rock, stared down at the sand. "She's asking them about their sex lives."

There was a long silence. He scuffed more sand.

"Well, what am I supposed to do about it? Steal her purse?"

"I want you to be interviewed."

When he finally glanced up, Laura was staring at him like he'd lost his mind. "You want me to have a job interview with your ex-wife, hoping she'll pick me for your next wife. Have I got that straight? It's not wind in my ear?"

"I don't care what you talk about, I just want you to keep her occupied while I figure out how to get her out of there. Please, I don't know what else to do. She's the most single-minded woman I know when she sets her sights on something."

"I know," Laura said into the wind. She glanced up at the lighted window. "Just look at her. She's like a shark going after a minnow."

Jack followed her gaze and had a perfect view of Cory, with her purse open, asking a pale-faced woman a question. "Oh, my God. That's no minnow, that's a church minister. This is an emergency. I'm begging you."

Laura laughed suddenly, her head thrown back so her chuckles were carried away on the wind. "You'd better not listen to the tape when I'm through, Jack. I'm planning to enjoy myself." She climbed swiftly up the stairs. Jack scrambled after her. In spite of his panic, he enjoyed the view of her gorgeously rounded rear swaying in front of him. Hell, at least the evening had some compensations.

They burst into the living room and moved in on Cory like a tag team.

"Reverend Eldred, how nice to see you," Jack said, giving the stunned woman his warmest smile. "Hasn't the weather been warm for this time of year?"

He stepped between her and Cory, moving the minister away so Laura could take her spot. "Have you seen the view from the dining room?" He led her off, trusting Laura to get him out of a jam.

"HI, CORY." Laura sent Jack's ex-wife a warm smile.

"Well, if it isn't Laura Kinkaide," the TV anchor-woman shouted into her right lapel.

Laura bit her lip. "I met your daughter, Sara, the other day. She certainly is a nice girl."

Cory's smile was genuine. "Thanks. I'm so proud of her. Jack's done a wonderful job."

"Hasn't he," Laura said sweetly. "He'll make some woman a fine husband."

"Is my lipstick straight?" Cory asked suddenly, flipping open her clutch purse. Laura could see her scanning the paper taped to the purse while she pretended to add fresh lipstick. Laura wondered how she'd ever let this woman intimidate her.

"So, you live in Seattle now," Cory stated. "And you have your own successful design business." Laura loved the way she raised her voice for key words she didn't want the tape to miss, like *Seattle,* and *design business.* "Do you ever think about moving back to Laroche?"

Laura leaned back and smoothed the red dress down toward her knees. She was going to enjoy herself. And if she managed a spot of revenge while she was doing Jack a favor, so much the better. "I would if I had a reason to."

"Like a man?" Her interviewer leaned forward eagerly.

"Among other things."

"You didn't mention a boyfriend in Seattle." Cory emphasized the word *boyfriend*.

"I'm recently single again." Laura sighed, glancing out the window, hoping she looked dejected and lonely. "I just haven't found the right guy in Seattle." She shrugged. "I guess I'm really a small-town girl at heart."

"I think giving up the sex is the hardest thing about being single, don't you?" Cory's lips were parted expectantly.

Laura looked around to make sure they couldn't be overheard. She saw Jack watching her from the other side of the room, and gave him a bright smile. "Frankly, since we're two single women talking here, alone where no one can hear us…"

Cory nodded eagerly.

"I can tell you, I miss sex so much I'm climbing the walls."

Her interviewer appeared pleased. She scanned down her list to the next question.

"And your religion is…?"

"You know, I hope you don't mind me saying this, seeing you used to be married to him and all, but I spend half my day at work fantasizing about Jack." Laura kept her voice strong and clear, and addressed her words to Cory's right lapel. She didn't want either of them to miss a word. "Just being under the same roof with him all day, I feel like I'm having hot flushes every time I see him." She flapped her hand under her chin. "Have you ever seen a guy fill a pair of jeans the way he does?"

"Really." Cory's eyes were glazing. She fumbled

with her purse. She seemed to have lost her place on the list.

"I was wondering...I can't help thinking... Oh, Cory, what's it like having sex with Jack?" Laura was the one leaning forward expectantly now.

Cory jerked back on the couch, blushing. She fiddled with her hair. "It was very nice. Uh, I'm not much of a cook. How about you—do you like cooking?"

"Nice? That's it?" Laura let huge disappointment seep into her tone.

Jack was still watching anxiously from across the room. Laura blew him a kiss. "Isn't he a good lover?"

"Really, Laura—"

"I was afraid of that." She shook her head sadly. "Sometimes those real good-looking types can be a big letdown when the lights go out and you get under the covers. You know what I mean? All bubbles and no fizz."

"Oh, *no*. Jack was always up for anything. Ha, ha. I mean...oh, gosh. Look at the time. I have to be out early tomorrow." She jumped up so fast her purse fell to the floor.

"As bad as that?" Laura sighed loudly, handing Cory her purse. "No wonder you left him."

Cory bolted for the door like a hunted animal.

"Oh, and Cory?"

"Yes?" She turned nervously.

"I'm Presbyterian. And I love cooking."

Cory giggled nervously and hurried on out the door.

Laura looked over at Jack, who threw his fist in the air and mouthed "Yes!"

Within seconds he was sitting in Cory's suddenly vacant spot on the couch.

"Great work, partner." She felt his smile right down to her squished toes. "How did you do that?"

Laura smiled back, helpless under the assault of those blue eyes. "I just told her what she wanted to hear." She chuckled softly. "And embellished a little."

"Thanks." He heaved a huge sigh of relief, stretching his long legs out in front of him. "I was getting ready to start packing and get out of Dodge before a lynch mob of angry women caught up with me."

She allowed herself a satisfied chuckle. Then asked the question she'd been wondering about. "Why is she doing this, Jack?"

"I don't know. She had some interview with an unhappy child actress and got the guilts. Not that they aren't overdue. But, like always, she had to go overboard. It would be nice if she came to see Sara more often. But that would get in the way of her career. Instead, she wants to find a substitute." He shrugged. "That's what she told me, anyway."

"I thought she wanted you back," Laura admitted.

Jack's face twisted in a grimace. "I thought so, too, till she laughed in my face and told me to lower my sights."

Laura touched his hand impulsively. She knew how it felt to love and lose someone. "I'm sorry, Jack."

He turned to her in surprise. "Sorry? Next to losing Sara, the worst thing that could happen to me would be living with Cory again." He tilted his head back. "I just hope she gives up this crazy idea of hers before there's trouble."

Laura opened her mouth, then shut it again.

He didn't want Cory back.

The truth took her breath away. She'd been so sure that all the elegant blond ex-cheerleader had to do was snap her fingers, and her discarded husband would be panting after her again. A small flame of warmth flickered inside now that Laura knew the truth.

After that, the evening just kept getting better.

JACK SPENT THE REST of the night by Laura's side. He fetched her dinner, and they sat together eating barbecued salmon and prawns with tiny new potatoes and assorted salads.

"This is delicious," Laura said as she bit into a succulent prawn. "Chip's quite the guy. Financial whiz by day, gourmet chef by night."

"Chip can't boil water," Jack assured her tersely. "He has these affairs catered."

Laura was still floating on air now she knew that Jack cared nothing for Cory. And, unless she was very much mistaken, he was showing all the signs of jealousy over Chip's sudden interest in her. She couldn't remember an evening she'd enjoyed more. "Still, Chip's been very nice to me. I'm looking forward to decorating his bedroom. He's told me I can do whatever I want in there."

"Just make sure it's decorating the *walls* he has in mind." Jack stabbed at his salmon. "Anyway, you have to finish the McNair House first."

After dinner, Chip put dancing deals together, pairing off his idea of likely candidates. Every time he came Laura's way Jack glared him down. Bruce Springsteen's

"Dancing in the Dark" came on, and Laura remembered the morning of the duelling CDs.

She glanced up at Jack, to find him smiling down at her, but something in the back of his eyes made her stomach flutter. "How 'bout we do it together this time?" he said, holding out his hand.

Laura put her hand in his and he led her to the dancing area. When he pulled her close, she felt the roughness of his cheek against hers, the hard warmth of his chest, the movement of his legs, which she followed instinctively. It was the first time they had ever danced together.

They were a perfect fit.

It felt so natural, there was a bittersweet ache in the back of her throat. Stan was right. There wasn't anything wrong with the men she dated. The problem was her heart wasn't free. It hadn't been free for a long time. She sighed and nestled closer to Jack, allowing his shoulder to cradle her head. Letting his warmth seep into her.

Jack murmured something in her ear, but she couldn't make out the words, only the primeval thrill caused by his warm breath stirring against her skin.

They danced to one song, then another. When the music changed tempo, Jack pulled away, saying gruffly, "Let's get out of here. I see Chip bearing down on you again."

Laura nodded and let him pull her by the hand away from the dancing couples and straight for the door. "Wait," she said. "I haven't got my purse."

"Where is it?"

"Chip's bedroom." She moved in that direction.

"I'll get it," Jack snapped. "You stay here." He almost sprinted to the bedroom, returning in seconds with the red clutch purse Gran had insisted on.

"But shouldn't we say goodbye to Chip?" Laura protested as he opened the door.

"I already did." As she opened her mouth, he quelled her with a glance. "From both of us."

Laura turned to hide the smile, making a mental note to phone Chip in the morning and thank him. In the meantime it was so nice to be treated like this by Jack. She was twenty-eight years old and felt, for the first time in her life, like the prom queen.

"Coat?" he asked.

She shook her head. She wasn't going to ruin the effect of her outfit by wearing the only coat she'd brought with her to Laroche. Better a few goose bumps than a bomber jacket with this dress.

The air was chilly on her bare arms as they stepped outside. She shivered slightly and Jack's leather jacket came round her.

"You'll need it yourself," she protested, even as her body snuggled into its warmth.

"We'll share," he said, putting his arm around her. She let herself lean into him, justifying the action as his need for warmth. She was tingling from head to toe, so aware of him, of the way their bodies moved in unison.

They came to her van first. Jack held on to her as they rounded the vehicle to the driver's side, then waited while she fished for her key and opened the door. She tried to give him his jacket back, but he stalled her with his hands on her arms. She opened her lips to argue and he stilled them with his mouth.

It was as though he'd been waiting all night to kiss her and he couldn't wait any longer. This was no quiet, chaste little kiss like the other night at the beach, either. This was a hungry, demanding kiss. A kiss of open mouths and exploring tongues. Laura discovered she had been waiting all night to kiss him, too, and joined in with enthusiasm.

As wet and vigorous as their teenage necking had been, this was adult kissing. Dimly, she noted how much his technique had improved, and how much better she liked the man's body he'd grown into. It felt so wonderful to touch him, to feel his hands moving on her back, over her hips, slow and sure.

He leaned back slightly, giving his hands room to move up her stomach and then to feather over her chest. She sighed with satisfaction, deep in her throat, as his hands soothed her aching breasts.

She let her own hands roam over the muscles of his back, his shoulders, his chest, reveling in the solid warmth of him, letting the sizzle of desire burst into flame.

When his hands traveled above her neckline, she noticed the calluses on his fingers and gloried in the rough texture on her sensitive skin. The sea-tinged air was cold on her overheated flesh, in sharp contrast to the heat she felt everywhere Jack touched her.

The gravel underfoot crunched as he shifted position. He trailed his lips down her neck, and she arched back against the cold metal of her van, giving him access that he greedily took advantage of. She ran her fingers through his thick hair, gasping as the cold air followed the wet path his mouth left down her neck and chest.

Then his hands were easing the zipper down her back, at the same time his teeth pulled the bodice down over her breasts until her tingling nipples were free to the air. She trembled all over at the knowledge that she was here in Jack's arms. That he'd chosen her—and that Cory had left the party alone.

As he took a nipple into his mouth, her head fell back and she gasped with the intensity of her desire, letting the delicious sensations wash over her, while thousands of stars winked down from a deep black sky. She felt like one of them, like a burning star herself in the cold night.

She wanted him with a fierceness she could no longer deny. For years she had pretended she was over him. But she wasn't. Probably never would be. As his mouth came back to hers for another deep kiss, she reached round and grabbed his hips, pulling him against her.

He groaned, deep in his throat, his own need apparent. Then suddenly jerked away.

"Get in the van," he whispered.

"The van?" Maybe her crush on him was as old as high school, but she wasn't a teenager any longer, and she certainly didn't plan on making out in the back of her dirty van in front of Chip's house.

Even as her desire-fogged mind tried to figure out an alternative, she realized Jack was pushing her into the driver's seat. That's when she noticed the door of Chip's house was wide-open, spilling out several couples and enough techno-pop music to deafen the local fish.

Suddenly the night wasn't theirs alone anymore. Voices broke the soft black stillness. Gravel crunched and scraped as steps drew closer to the line of cars. Laughing comments were exchanged. Jack swiftly zipped the jacket up over her sagging dress, cursing under his breath.

She was stunned with the force of their mutual desire as well as by the abrupt way it was cut off. She could only sit there, dazed, wanting him.

With a crooked smile he leaned through the open door. "Are you okay to drive?"

She nodded.

"Meet me back at my place. Sara's still at your Gran's," he whispered, half urgent, half pleading.

But already common sense was intruding on her blissful fantasy. She shook her head, unable to look at him. "No, this is..." How to explain the deadly mix of emotion and pure flaming lust that raged within her?

She was too vulnerable to Jack. Too easily hurt. One voice inside her ordered caution, even as another clamored to be allowed to see this thing through once and for all.

Caution won.

"No, I can't," she cried breathlessly, forcing her body to turn around and her shaking fingers to insert the key into the ignition.

She felt his frustration in his labored breathing. He kicked at the gravel with his boot. When he spoke his voice was bitter, angry. "I'm not going to say I'm sorry, because I'm not. If that dork you're going out with had any brains, he'd be down here taking care of you."

Laura felt like he'd slapped her. "What do you mean, taking care of me?" She swung her head round.

For answer, he grabbed her face and kissed her hard.

"We would be fantastic together, and you know it." He rose in one fluid motion and stomped off down the gravel road to his truck.

She sat there for a full minute, letting her own frustration level drop and trying to get her pulse under control. She also wanted Jack to get going ahead of her so he and Sara would be gone when she returned to Gran's house.

She fixed her dress, combed her hair and dabbed on fresh lipstick.

No lights came on behind her.

She turned on the engine, started the heater, then glanced in the rearview mirror and saw his headlights. Laura waited, listening to the idling of another engine, but no truck pulled out.

Finally she realized he was waiting for her to go first. Which she did, gritting her teeth and muttering curses against overbearing, interfering men.

Laura glanced into the rearview mirror once she got on the highway, and there he was, right behind her. It annoyed her so much she shoved the mirror to an impossible angle just so she wouldn't have to watch Jack follow her all the way home.

She parked the van outside her grandmother's house and let herself in the front door. She shrugged off Jack's coat, leaving it on the coat rack in the entrance hall. By the time she'd done that and crossed to the kitchen where Gran and Sara were playing cards, she could hear Jack coming in behind her.

"Have a nice time, dear?" Gran said.

"That dress is way cool," Sara said.

"Laura, could I speak to you?" Jack said, barging into the kitchen.

"Wonderful, thanks, and no," Laura replied.

She turned to fill the kettle, thinking a cup of chamomile tea would calm her and help her sleep. Her sixth sense told her Jack was behind her before she felt his hand on her shoulder.

"Laura, please let's not leave it this way," he said softly, so only she could hear.

Unaccountably, her eyes filled with tears. Feeling foolish, and determined not to let him see her weakness, she brushed past him and out the door, almost running up the stairs. Not until she was safely locked in the bathroom with the tap running did she give in to a fit of sobbing.

Long after she heard the truck drive away she stayed in the bathroom, crying.

The damned stupid truth was that she loved him. Oh, she'd always loved him. But in Seattle she'd built a life that had thick walls to protect her heart. Back in Laroche, in just a couple of weeks, Jack had bulldozed those carefully built walls and exposed her vulnerable lovesick heart. Just for the pleasure of breaking it all over again.

"We'd be fantastic together and you know it," he'd whispered. Well, he was right; she did know it. She also knew that an affair with him would devastate her when they had to part. And she wasn't going to let that happen.

There was only one way to make sure she wasn't a victim of Jack's destructive charm again.

Leave town.

7

"SO YOU'RE RUNNING AWAY again." Gran's voice hit Laura like a slap. Laura turned from the open suitcase with a guilty start, to see her grandmother standing in the doorway, her expression stony in the morning light.

"I'm not..." Laura began. Then, unable to turn from the truth, she let her head drop. "I have to run away. Call it self-preservation."

"I call it cowardice." Gran's matter-of-fact tone hurt more than any yelling would. "You love that boy. Face it, Laura. Running won't change the way you feel."

No, but it would stop her from getting tangled up any more than she already was, physically and emotionally.

"Please try to understand, Gran." Laura sank down on the bed. She could barely hold back the tears. "I have to go."

The old woman shook her head sadly. "I've never seen two people more perfect for each other who went about the business so badly." She sighed noisily. "And what about the McNair House?"

"They'll find somebody else. I'll send a fax when I get back to Seattle. I'll leave the supplies and all my design sheets for the next person. I can even suggest some good designers who could finish the job."

"Humph." Gran turned away and plonked down the

stairs to the kitchen, where Laura soon heard pots banging while she finished packing.

The heavy suitcase clunked down the stairs behind her. When she reached the main level, the smell of blueberry pancakes made her smile in spite of her misery. It was a smell that took Laura back to childhood. For a special treat—or to make her feel better after any kind of setback—Gran always made blueberry pancakes.

Laura didn't want breakfast. She wanted to get in her van and put miles between her and Jack as quickly as possible. But she couldn't hurt Gran's feelings. She dumped the suitcase by the front door and returned to the kitchen. Silently, she set the table and poured coffee. Gran put a stack of pancakes in front of her and sat opposite to enjoy her own dwarf stack.

Laura still didn't want breakfast. But the butter melting in a golden puddle on top of the pancakes made her mouth water. When she poured the amber maple syrup into the butter, the larger pool overflowed in rivulets.

The first bite was so delicious the world didn't seem quite so terrible anymore. She glanced up at Gran.

"Don't leave today, dear. It's Sunday. You wouldn't be working, anyway. Take a little rest and think about things. If you still feel the same way tomorrow, you can telephone Delores Walters and inform her in person of your decision to quit."

Laura took another big bite, taking time to think while her mouth was full. Surely she owed Gran this much. She chewed and swallowed. She nodded. "But don't try and stop me tomorrow."

She lugged her suitcase back upstairs, then helped Gran prepare the vegetables for dinner.

"Do you want to come with me to church?"

"No thanks, Gran. I think I'll walk up to the McNair House and see if I've left anything there I can't live without."

The older woman nodded. "If you're going up there anyway, you can take some old bedding I'm loaning to the place."

The "old bedding" was a faded, hand-stitched quilt in a double wedding ring pattern. The original colors were probably dark reds and blues, Laura guessed, but time had mellowed them to shades of soft rose and Wedgewood. The quilt spoke of a time when women worked together to sew an heirloom gift for a new bride. Laura traced one of the rings. "I've never seen this before. It's beautiful."

"Some of the neighbors made it for my mother's wedding. You can see where they've stitched their names on the back. Mother passed it to me when I married. I intended to give it to your mother but—" Gran shrugged eloquently "—her marriage bed was in the back of a van. And she's never been the homemaker type. So I've been saving it for you."

Sharp eyes turned on Laura. "But the way you're carrying on, it'll be years before it's needed. Until then it seems a shame to keep it in the attic, when visitors to Laroche could enjoy a real piece of local history. I typed the names of the women who made it—the list is right here in the box. Perhaps the committee could make a little plaque to go over the bed. I'll suggest it at the meeting Wednesday night."

The meeting Laura wouldn't be attending. She touched the quilt reverently, moved by the sense of family and community it represented. Also in the box was a set of delicately embroidered linen sheets and pillowcases. Gran had even included two feather pillows. Not original, she informed Laura, but the kind her mother used.

"You should take these up when the rest of the house is ready. They might get dusty," Laura protested.

Gran shook her head. "I want you to put them on the bed and see if they fit. We might need to make some alterations."

So Laura lugged the lavender-scented box into the McNair House. It was heavy enough without the burden of guilt she was carrying along with it. She should have quit the minute she found out Jack was also working on the house. Now she was letting Gran and Delores Walters and the others down.

Delivering the treasure box of antique linens just made her feel worse—like a depressing old spinster donating her untouched trousseau to a museum. Which, when she came to think about it, was exactly the case. Laura hauled the box up the stairs and down the hall into the master bedroom.

The old mattress hadn't been salvageable, but the replacement mattress was already on the big old fourposter.

Laura took her time making the bed. Tears pricked her eyes as she tucked the sheets carefully around the mattress. She slipped the embroidered cases over the pillows and then shook the quilt out and floated it onto the bed. The smell of lavender hung in the air.

There was an ache deep inside her as she thought of the two brides who had first made love under this quilt.

Both had enjoyed long, successful marriages. Laura had a sudden vision of herself and Jack in that bed, under that quilt, and the pain of longing made her bite hard on her lip to ward off another crying jag.

She turned resolutely away and walked to the other side of the room, where the cabbage rose stencil leaned against the wall. Memory hit her anew.

She saw herself and Sara working happily together, and relived that curious moment when she and Jack had stared at each other across the room, communicating in a way they never managed with mere words. She picked up the stencil and then changed her mind, putting it back again. The next designer might want to repeat the motif somewhere else.

Her footsteps echoed loudly in the quiet house as she toured the upstairs rooms, picking up the odd forgotten paintbrush, her level, an Exacto knife. She felt like an artist abandoning her masterpiece half-done. Would the next designer follow her design boards? Would they understand how important it was to put a touch of gilt on this molding? Would they find the right drapery fabric?

She hated unfinished business. And this house meant so much to her.

But her safety meant more.

She and Jack also had unfinished business, and if she was to preserve her sanity, she needed to leave it unfinished. Which meant leaving town. Because now she had tasted his kisses again, felt his hands on her body. She shuddered as the memory of the wild passion she'd felt in his arms intruded. And she was terrified that, if she followed her heart's desire, she would end up burned to a cinder by her own passion.

She trod back down the stairs, letting her fingers trail along the mahogany stair rail, wishing she hadn't come back.

She felt his presence before she reached the bottom of the steps, and turned instinctively into the front parlor, where Jack was crouched in front of the fireplace, carving a new section of mantel.

She heard the whisper of metal scraping against wood as she moved silently into the room. Jack's concentration was evident in every line of his taut back, in the way he held his head. Even his breathing was slow and controlled.

Laura watched an arc of paper-thin wood build behind him as he worked a chisel in one smooth motion. His other hand followed its path, and Laura shivered, remembering those hands moving with the same concentration last night when he'd traced the curve of her body from hip to breast.

He turned slowly to look at her, even though she was sure she hadn't made a sound. His eyes quietly assessed her, asking questions Laura didn't want to answer. She wanted to turn and run, but her body was paralyzed, helpless to follow the primal urge to escape the predator.

Jack rose slowly and came to stand a few feet away.

She willed herself not to blush.

"Hi." His eyes searched her face.

"Hi." She backed up a step.

"I'm sorry about last night." He gazed down at the chisel still in his hands and rubbed its surface as though checking for sharpness. "I hope we can still work together...." There was a small pause, during which Jack glanced up, then back down again as if fascinated by the tool in his hands.

Laura's brain and mouth remained paralyzed. Adrenaline spurted through her body. Her heart was banging away on overdrive, but like a flooded engine, her brain had stalled. And she couldn't seem to move.

"But, if you want me to, I'll quit the project," he said at last. He looked uncomfortable, as if he wished last night had never happened.

Laura's brain roared to life. Well, he wasn't the only one who wished it hadn't happened. But did he think she was still a sixteen-year-old who couldn't handle a kiss without falling in love?

Okay, so she was, but she had no intention of letting him know that.

His assumption that they could no longer work together made her furious, and that made her foolhardy. She wasn't finished with the nicest piece of work she'd done in her career. Why should she walk away from the Mona Lisa before she'd painted the smile?

Because of Jack? Oh, no. Maybe she wasn't going anywhere, after all.

"Relax, Jack." Her voice sounded confident and steady. "It was just a kiss." She saw his look of astonishment, saw his lips open, and hurried on. "A...a kiss that got a bit out of hand. It was a mistake, but it won't happen again. Really," she said to his rapidly flushing face, "it's no big deal."

She smiled, watching his male ego deflate. "I'll see you tomorrow."

She had the satisfaction of knowing she'd knocked his pride down a mile or two. It was only after she'd started the van and was on her way back to Gran's that she realized she had just told Jack she wasn't quitting. It was one thing to brazen it out for a couple of minutes, but she couldn't keep up the act for long. She felt just like that lovesick teenager again.

Maybe worse.

Laura banged her fist on the steering wheel, "Stupid, stupid, stupid." She'd backed herself into a tight corner, but, as Stan was fond of telling her, she was an expert at avoiding intimacy. She calmed down and decided to put most of her energy into finishing her masterpiece. And a little bit of energy into making sure she and the sexy carpenter worked in different parts of the house.

GRAN, PREDICTABLY, refused to show excitement when Laura announced she was staying, after all. They ate a pleasant Sunday-night roast dinner together while she picked her grandmother's brains about any local lore that had been handed down with the quilt. That got Gran reminiscing, telling Laura not her own familiar stories, but the remembered stories of her own mother, Laura's great-grandmother.

Soon Laura was picturing Laroche's pioneer women in starched dresses and piled-up hair. Women who brought their own ideas of civilization to this little speck of a town on an island flung past the edge of the wilderness.

Here, they'd bullied the men into building churches. They'd preached temperance, made jellies of the summer fruits and given birth in their own beds to the next generation of builders and reformers.

Her great-grandmother had been a friend of Mrs. McNair, and Laura imagined her ancestor sitting with the original owner of the McNair House in the parlor, having tea.

Her history, the house's history—they insisted on overlapping.

After dinner, she pulled out her design pad and started doodling, playing with ideas for the nursery and servants' quarters on the third floor. It would be a fairly quick job, as only a portion of the third floor would be open to the public. And, in keeping with authenticity, there wouldn't be much decorating or furnishing to be done.

What Laura really wanted was to start work on the main floor rooms, which posed by far the greatest challenge. But Jack was still working there, and until he was finished, Laura didn't want to go near it. After that, he would go down into the basement kitchen and then... She flicked through her design sheets and found the ones for the main floor.

They were dense with sketches, scribbles, scraps of paper and fabric. Stan had called her about a horsehair parlor set that was coming up for auction, and Laura, in a burst of enthusiasm, had not only promised to attend next weekend's auction in Seattle, but had sketched the set onto her design sheet.

IT'S NO BIG DEAL. The words spun round and round in Jack's head. He couldn't concentrate on the intricate carving he had to copy.

He'd hardly slept the night before; his body so on fire for Laura it physically hurt him. No woman had ever affected him like this. He tried to pass it off as the frustration of an aroused man who hadn't had a woman in a while, but by the small hours of the dark night Jack knew that wasn't true. It wasn't just his body that cried out for Laura. It was some part of him that she made whole.

He knew she'd been upset when she first drove away. He could understand that she might be angry with him for trying to seduce her in a gravel parking lot. Maybe she was mad at herself for fooling around on her boyfriend. Jack appreciated that as well. Or maybe she just didn't think they should work together and sleep together.

By dawn he'd decided that if he quit the project, they could start over, take it slowly. He knew a few guys he could trust to do most of the remaining work, all except the hand carving. If he and Laura didn't work together, that was one objection taken care of. Then all he had to do was make damn sure they weren't in a parking lot the next time he made a move.

Oh, yeah. And she'd have to dump the boyfriend.

He was prepared to deal with all her objections. But "no big deal"? If she hadn't been shaken to the core by what had happened between them, then she'd put on a pretty damn good act.

He'd had his fair share of sex; he'd known passion and the kind of pleasure that puts a smile on your face for days. But something else leaped to life when he and Laura started touching each other—something that scared him.

He had a feeling she could take him to heights he'd never imagined. And when she left this island that still held him prisoner, would do until Sara finished school, Laura might just take his happiness with her.

He was still willing to take that risk. Their little escapade in the parking lot felt like it had changed Jack forever. And to her it was "no big deal"?

He recalled her face this morning when she'd said those words to him. It had been strained and pale. Dark circles had smudged her eyes. Now that he thought about it, she'd looked like a woman who hadn't slept at all last night. He could look in the mirror and see the same signs.

He started to smile.

She was lying.

"No big deal." *Ha.* He'd like to show Laura a "big deal." He'd like that very much. He rubbed the stubble on his chin thoughtfully. That boyfriend of hers hadn't been anywhere near Laura since she'd come to Laroche, he was sure of it. She never even talked about him. The guy, Peter or whatever his name was, had left the field wide-open as far as Jack was concerned. Laura wasn't as cool as she pretended to be; he'd bet his Joe Montana autographed football on that.

It was like a black cloud had just lifted and the world was bathed in sunshine again. If Laura was having sleepless nights over him, she was vulnerable. On the football team, Jack had always liked playing offense. He enjoyed observing his opponents' weaknesses and working out a strategy to get through their defenses and score. Yep, this was no football match, but he definitely intended to score. And like any match where victory was important, he needed a very careful game plan.

First, he had to prepare the field. A seduction scene was definitely required. If they'd been somewhere quiet and private last night, instead of making out on the road like a couple of horny kids, he wouldn't have spent the night burning with frustration.

He would have finished what he and Laura had started.

He would have spent the night learning her body, exploring all her secret places, making her cry out loud with pleasure.

Next time, he'd be prepared—he'd use every dirty trick ever perfected by man to get woman in the sack.

He'd better get some champagne and soft music, all that stuff women liked. He chuckled softly, beginning to savor his plan. Next, he needed a quiet location with lots of privacy. That was more difficult. His house gave him the home-team advantage, but was out of the question because of Sara. Laura's was equally impossible because of Gran.

He paced the floor, hearing the lonely echo of his boots in the empty room.

He could have hit himself over the head with the chisel for his stupidity. Of course, he was *in* the perfect location. The McNair House.

A surge of excitement coursed through him. Jack played to win. Laura had scored points in the last encounter, but he knew some of her weak spots. Like that soft place under her ear. When he touched it with his tongue, she shivered clear down to her toes.

He smiled in memory.

He'd found one or two of her weak spots. He was going to find plenty more and exploit them ruthlessly. This game was too important to mess up—Jack wanted them both to win.

Dragging out the small, leather-bound notebook he always carried in his back pocket, he flipped to the current page. Under "seasoned mahogany, 1X8," he wrote "champagne" and "glasses."

He thought about the primitive conditions in the kitchen and added "bucket, ice, candles."

He tapped his teeth with his pencil. Scribbled "condoms." He closed his eyes, wondering what else to add to the list, then practiced a few mental run-throughs, picturing the scene. He was feeling aroused already.

He imagined lying with Laura afterward. If last night was any indication, he expected a splendid, vigorous workout. Sex always made him hungry.

He added "snacks" to the list.

Whistling his own personal victory chant, he ran up the stairs and did a quick reconnoitre. He almost laughed out loud when he saw the bed already made up in the master bedroom. He felt like his team was already on the scoreboard.

Jack was still whistling, his mood considerably lighter, when he returned downstairs. He was able to give the right concentration to the intricate detail he was carving. It left part of his mind free for the equally intricate details of what he planned to do to Laura once he had her naked in that big bed upstairs.

He'd left Cory at home with Sara, trying to catch up on a year's growth and activities in one day. He was happy to give mother and daughter time alone together now he knew Cory didn't plan to take Sara away.

He left for home in the late afternoon, as promised, for his recap meeting with Cory, so they could go over her candidates for his new wife. He wondered what she'd made of the night before. And what Laura had said to her.

He really wanted to hear that tape.

When he got home, Cory and Sara were curled up in front of the TV watching a movie and eating microwave popcorn. So much for mother-daughter intimacy. Had they run out of conversation already? As soon as she saw him, Cory left Sara in front of the TV and joined him in the kitchen with a buff file folder in her hands.

He grabbed a soda from the fridge, offering one to Cory, who shook her head. She sat down across from him at the kitchen table and flipped open the folder.

"Is my wife in there?" He gestured with the pop can.

"It was a disappointing turnout last night," Cory replied. "I've tallied the results, but I don't think our work is done yet." She seemed dispirited.

"I thought there were lots of nice women at Chip's party. What did you think of Mary, the bank manager?" He sipped soda from the can, keeping his eyes innocent, watching Cory as she flipped through a stack of printed pages.

She found what she was looking for and scanned the page. She shook her head. "Too hostile."

"The teacher?"

She consulted her notes. "Too high-strung."

"How about Laura?"

Cory didn't even need her notes for that one, just

stared at him as if he was out of his mind for asking. "That woman's obsessed by sex, Jack. It's not healthy."

He choked on his soda. "Did she tell you about this, uh, problem?"

"It was all she could talk about." Cory's cheeks flushed. "She had the nerve to ask me if you were a good lover."

He rocked back in his chair, a slow smile forming. "Was I?"

"I'm not here to pander to your ego, Jack. I got the impression Laura didn't think you'd be man enough for her."

"What?" The chair banged to the floor. He bolted straight up, no longer amused.

"Frankly, I think she's a nymphomaniac." Cory snapped the folder shut. "No, we'll have to keep looking. Maybe we should take out a personal ad."

"What about her boyfriend in Seattle? Does he satisfy her?"

"Whose boyfriend?"

"Laura's!"

She thinned her lips in a disapproving expression, flicking through the notes again. "No boyfriend. They broke up before she started this job."

His heart gave a funny lurch. "Are you sure? You didn't mix her up with somebody else?"

"I'm sure. She talked about how being single was driving her crazy, because of having to do without...you know. Anyway, you can forget about Laura. She's one sick puppy. Do you want me to write the ad?"

Things were definitely looking up. No boyfriend left the playing field a little less crowded. And she'd thrown out yet another challenge. Didn't think he'd be man enough for her, huh? He remembered how she'd smiled and waved at him while she was being interviewed. She was definitely not playing by the rules, taunting him like that. He'd have to think up a special penalty.

He realized his ex-wife was still waiting for an answer. "Let me think about it. I appreciate all you've done. Let's leave it for a bit."

Cory looked at him severely. "Sara's getting older every day. And so are you." She pushed her chair back. "I'll call you next weekend. We'll talk then."

"Um, something's been bothering me. What were you expecting on the fax machine at your hotel?"

"What?" Cory scratched her head. "Oh, some interview questions for a show I'm taping next week."

A light came on in Jack's head. "Interview questions? Do you mean other people usually write your questions for you?"

She looked puzzled at his sudden interest. "Well sure, we have researchers who put together backgrounders on our subjects and write questions."

She must have read the amusement in his face. Maybe she knew he was thinking about the mess she'd made of her interviews at Chip's house. "Of course, I can do it myself, I'm just so busy with other things." She sounded defensive, and her cheeks were reddening under her makeup.

So she still used cheat sheets. Jack smiled to himself. Some things didn't change.

JACK WAS ALREADY AT WORK, whistling cheerfully, when Laura arrived Monday morning. He gave her a smile so warm it bordered on animal.

"You should bottle and sell that mood of yours. You'd make a fortune," Laura grumbled. *And she'd be first in line to buy a bottle.* Jack had obviously forgotten all about their little scene the other night. Just what her ego needed.

She meant to stomp on up the stairs, but her eyes were drawn to what Jack was doing. Professional curiosity pushed her forward to watch him carving the details into the new section of the wooden mantel. "You couldn't save the original?" Laura asked. She was a purist, after all.

He shook his head. "Woodworm."

She'd seen a lot of man-made beauty literally eaten away by nature's busy little recyclers. "Did they get much else?"

"Some paneling, I think. Nothing too drastic. Luckily, the city's kept the house up ever since it took the property over."

She stood by his side watching, fascinated, as he carved, using woodworking tools like an artist's brushes. She bent closer, admiring his technique as he added details to a head emerging from carved oak leaves. She heard the soft scrape of metal on wood as a mythical face began to emerge.

She felt the heat from his body, breathed in the scent of wood and a whiff of something citrusy. "The green man?" she asked.

He nodded. "A favorite subject for carvers—the spirit of the tree peeking out through the branches." He stopped to wipe the sawdust away with a rag, leaned back and squinted at his work. "Although in this case, I'd guess whoever carved this mantel just copied it from a picture of an English fireplace."

He shrugged at her raised eyebrows. "It feels English."

So he had them, too. Those unexplained hunches. As she watched him work, she saw the artistry in what he did. He could call himself a carpenter, but he was a true craftsman. She wondered if even she would be able to tell which half was new and which was the original when he'd finished.

The smell of new wood, mixed with the spicy fragrance of the man next to her, was intoxicating. She should move on, keep to her resolution to stay out of temptation's way. But she lingered.

"Who taught you to do that?" she asked softly.

"Your grandfather. Remember how I used to follow him around? He carved all kinds of things. Furniture, animals, the odd piece of missing trim from one of the old houses around here. He'd talk to me sometimes or, more often, listen to me talk. Then he started teaching me. He was a wonderful man, your grandpa."

"Yes." Suddenly she did remember the young Jack helping Grandpa in his shed. She'd always found the intricate wood carving a real bore to watch, but Jack had been fascinated. And had helped carry on a hand-crafting tradition. "He'd be very proud if he could see you now."

Jack glanced up at her then, their eyes only inches apart. He smiled, and there was something in that smile that made Laura's heart speed up. Some disturbing message in the deep-blue eyes that warned of danger.

She was getting that fight or flight response again and frankly didn't know whether to attack him or run like hell.

She straightened. "I'd better get started."

"Are you in the master bedroom today?" Jack asked casually.

"No, I'm pretty much finished in there. I'm starting on the third floor maid's room."

"Oh." He sounded disappointed.

8

ALL LAURA'S RESEARCH made her glad she wasn't a maid living in the late nineteenth century. She rolled pale-green paint on the walls and the ceiling in the tiny attic bedroom. No fancy paint finishes here. She hoped to find a single metal bed and a simple chest of drawers. A few hooks were still hanging on the wall, all the poor maid had for a closet.

Laura managed to drizzle as much paint onto her hair, clothing and the canvas drop cloths as she rolled onto the ceiling. She was sticky, hot and half-choked with fumes from the oil-based paint when a voice made her jump.

"My God, it's the creature from the black lagoon," Jack cried in mock alarm from the doorway.

"Ha! My next victim!" Laura snarled at him, holding her green roller out like a weapon.

"I come in peace, bearing gifts," he retorted, holding out the coffee thermos. She put the roller down gratefully.

He walked in and made a face. "Smells like you're waging chemical warfare in here." He stepped forward and touched the tip of his index finger to the side of her nose. "And losing." He smiled, holding his green-tipped finger up to her, his eyes as blue and twinkling as the waves of Laroche harbor on a sunny day.

Her heart lurched.

He wiped his finger on her multisplattered denim shoulder. It could have been boiling oil he was rubbing into her the way the simple gesture seared her. "Why don't we go down to one of the finished rooms and have coffee?" He started to back away, but Laura stopped him.

"I can't go anywhere until I'm dry. You go ahead, I'll have mine in here."

"No. I'll stay with you." He looked around the room. "Is there anything we can lean on?"

"I haven't painted the door yet."

"You're asking me to shut the single source of ventilation?"

"Look, you don't have to stay."

He shut the door and sank to the floor.

Laura smiled down at him. "I did open the window." She gestured to the open pane high up one wall.

Jack handed her a mug, and belatedly she realized she'd have to sit either squished up beside him or in the middle of the room. Her neck was hurting from painting the ceiling. She needed to lean on something. Gingerly, she sat down beside Jack.

"Watch your elbows," she warned, pulling her body in tight. There wasn't much space between them and the wet walls. As small as she tried to make herself, Laura couldn't help but touch Jack. His body was warm and solid, setting her nerve endings buzzing everywhere their bodies met.

She drank thankfully from the yellow mug, trying to ignore the enforced intimacy. "You make great coffee."

He turned to her in surprise. "You really think so?"

"Mmm."

"Huh."

She rolled her shoulders.

"You're going to have to ditch the Michelangelo act until your neck gets better," he said.

He put his coffee cup down, and before she could stop him, he'd picked her up bodily and hauled her onto his lap. She didn't dare struggle because of the paint. "Put me down," she gasped. "Jack, you'll get paint all over yourself."

He opened his legs and she bumped to the ground. "Now hold still." His magic fingers started moving on her neck in the wonderful way she remembered, and suddenly all the fight went out of her.

"There's a girl in Sara's class who has her hair streaked with green just like this. Very fashionable." His voice teased gently, while the rolling pressure on her neck and shoulders was too soothing to resist. His touch, like his tone, was light, friendly, with no threatening undertones. As a ploy to avoid intimacy, Laura mused, dousing herself in paint seemed to be quite effective.

She relaxed.

Being held against him, feeling the heat of his thighs against the outside of hers, the warmth of his hands, was all so familiar, so right. He rubbed her neck for a long time while she let herself lean against him, her eyes drifting shut.

His hands were callused, working hands. She thought she felt a hint of papery sawdust as he rubbed her skin. Above the sharp odor of paint she could smell the new-wood scent that clung to his fingers and clothing. His breathing was slow and deliberate, like the movement of his hands. Each breath out caused a waft of warm air on the back of her neck like the whisper of a caress.

She didn't know when the atmosphere started to change, but suddenly she didn't feel so relaxed. A new and different kind of tension began to build. And for all her plans to stay aloof, she was powerless to move.

Still, she figured, it wasn't like she was in her sexy red dress with her makeup intact and her hair done. He'd just told her she resembled something out of a horror film.

Only a man desperate, or deeply in love, could find a paint-globbed, work-boot-shod, sweat-stained woman a big turn-on. She'd seen the way women were looking at Jack at the party the other night. He was too good-looking, too confident, to be desperate.

She wished quite suddenly that she *was* wearing something sexy and her makeup was flawless. Perhaps she would turn her head and let her rouged lips float by his. Let him get a whiff of her perfume and a glimpse of cleavage until he was helplessly in her thrall.

For she realized that she wanted him any way she could get him. Better a little bit of heaven now than a lifetime of wondering...and wishing. At least, when she packed her broken heart, she would also have a treasure box of memories to take along.

She didn't know when the movement of Jack's hands changed to a caress; she only knew that it did. Instead of jumping away, like she'd planned, she sighed with a mixture of gratitude and anticipation.

His lips whispered over the back of her neck, making

her shiver. He kissed the flesh under her right earlobe, trailing his tongue in a lazy circle and, just like that, she felt the hot, slick rush of desire slide through her body.

Snap, snap—he released the denim straps on her overalls. She clutched the knees on either side of her own and her heart thudded. As though seeking to sooth that overworked organ, he trailed his hands down her T-shirt and over her heart, which only beat more crazily.

She never bothered with a bra when she wore her overalls, so there was nothing between her breasts and his seductive hands but a bit of flimsy cotton, and her nipples felt like they were doing their best to burst through the T-shirt. They literally ached for his touch. But he made her wait, tracing the shape of her over and over again through the cloth.

By the time he slid his fingers under the shirt, she was panting and helpless. His leathery hands climbed lazily up her belly before finally cupping her breasts. She moaned as he pinned each nipple between two fingers.

She turned her face to him then, and kissed him with her unrouged lips, slow and deep. He didn't seem to mind that she was a mess, but kissed her back with an intensity that made her quiver. His hands came out of her T-shirt and she heard the tinny sound as he popped the rest of the snaps on her overalls. Each metallic ping sent another shiver of excitement curling up her spine.

She felt like she'd been waiting twelve years for this moment—and she couldn't wait another second.

She turned her body fully around to face him and dove forward, plunging her fingers into the thick waves of his hair. Her lips seemed to telegraph their message of need and urgency as their mouths met again.

The tempo picked up immediately.

He left her mouth only long enough to yank her T-shirt up and over her head. When their lips met again, her naked breasts were pressed against the chambray of his shirt. She rubbed herself against him, feeling the soft fabric, the scratchiness of sawdust and the hard scrape of buttons on her flesh, while his tongue teased and tormented her mouth.

He pulled back, breathing heavily, to gaze at her naked torso. The expression on his face made her feel beautiful.

Kneeling before him, Laura unbuttoned his workshirt, laughing as bits of sawdust flew through the air when she popped each button. She ran her fingers over the muscular chest with its mat of copper hair, leaving streaks of green behind, while he yanked the rest of his shirt off and threw it into the middle of the room.

Both kneeling now, they came together, naked chest to naked chest, mouth-to-mouth. Laura clutched him to her, needing him in the deepest part of her. Her body cried out for him, and with her tongue and her roving hands, she let him feel her need. She refused to think, refused to do anything but feel the glorious sensations. He tugged, and the sagging overalls slid down over her hips.

"Wait, my boots..." she mumbled. She sat down on her cotton panties. The bulky denim was puddled at her ankles, trapped there by the brown bulk of leather and metal. Jack unlaced each steel-toed boot as though it were a dancing slipper, and carefully eased each foot out.

Next he drew off her gray woollen work socks, and finally he pulled the overalls off her legs. Her eyes fell to his jeans, and he obeyed her silent command, unzipping and yanking at them while she unlaced his boots, removed his own wool socks. Somewhere outside a car honked, the noise strangely out of place in the panting silence of the maid's room.

Jack leaned behind her and she watched the play of his athlete's muscles as he wadded a tarpaulin before tipping her back on it. The material was scratchy under her naked skin, and cool and sticky where she landed on squishy dollops of congealing paint.

"I feel like I'm in a mud wrestling match," she groaned.

His eyes were alight with laughter as he rolled on top of her, warm and pulsing with vitality. "Honey, I think you're losing."

She smiled back at him, feeling crazy and wicked and more alive than she'd ever felt in her life. She groped with one hand until she felt the paint tray. Dipping her fingers in the green ooze, she said, "Don't be too sure," and rubbed it into his chest, until he looked like he was decorated with Spanish moss.

"I'd return the favor except I don't want to get chemical poisoning when I take my tongue to your breasts," he whispered.

His eyes roved over her in a way that make her heart stop beating. He nuzzled her neck, trailed kisses to her breasts and kissed and suckled her there until she gasped, grabbing his head to press him to her.

He dropped kisses over her belly, dipping his tongue into her navel, making her giggle. His gaze fastened on the cotton panties, and with a little growl he took the waistband between his teeth. He slipped a hand under her hips, which she obligingly raised. Then, using his teeth to pull from the front, rather like a dog worrying a bone, and his hand to pull from the back, he slipped her panties down and all the way off.

She lay there naked and exposed while he knelt beside her, looking his fill. "You are the most beautiful thing I've ever seen." His voice was husky.

His fingers trembled slightly as he reached for the tangle of curls he'd just uncovered.

She caught her breath as he touched her, dipped a finger inside her and trailed the wetness up to the throbbing bud. He lay down beside her and kissed her again, while his fingers danced slowly upon her until she was writhing helplessly in his arms.

"Wait," she panted, knowing her explosion was imminent. "I want you inside me."

He ripped his briefs off in a tearing hurry, then crawled naked to the heaped denim and dragged out his jeans, fumbling in the pocket until he found a square plastic packet.

Then he was on top of her and she opened her legs to him. He placed himself at the entrance, pausing to stare deep into her eyes.

She gazed back for a long moment, seeing his need, letting him see her own. It was like going back in time to when he was her hero, the pinnacle of her dreams. And yet it was not. There were a dozen years of growing up and experience between them. It was all reflected in their eyes—the memories, the regrets.

But most of all, the wanting.

When she could bear the painful intimacy of his gaze

no longer, she pulled his head down for his kiss. As their lips met, he surged into her, and she felt she would burst with the pleasure of it.

She clasped him to her, wrapping him with her legs, hugging him with her arms and kissing him with her lips, her tongue. With each thrust it felt as though he were going deeper into her, penetrating her most secret places, and she opened each of them to him gladly.

He filled her body completely, taking her higher and higher until she was swept away. She cried out as her body clenched with ecstasy again and again. Like an echo, she heard Jack cry out his own pleasure.

They lay, entwined and spent, for a long time, listening to each other's breathing slow. "From now on, every time I smell paint, I'll think of you naked," he said.

"We'll need to shower in turpentine," she chuckled.

His hand wandered over the mottled green flesh that stretched from her shoulder to her belly. "I like you just like this. You're a work of art, my painted lady."

Her heart swelled with love and she hugged him fiercely. She tried to roll on top of him, but the tarpaulin came with her, glued to her back. "Ouch," she cried out, as he gingerly pulled the offending fabric away.

"Come on," he said, pulling Laura to her feet. "Get dressed, we're going to my house to clean up."

They dressed swiftly, making faces as the clothing stuck to paint patches on their skin, then jumped into his truck for the short drive to Jack's house.

Laura sat beside him, feeling like she was back in her childish make-believe world again, pretending Jack was her husband. For now, it was enough. They didn't talk, but they never stopped touching. His right hand clasped her left thigh possessively, while Laura drew patterns on his shirt with one fingertip.

When they reached Jack's house, he ushered her inside and directed her to the bathroom. "I'll be right back with the turpentine," he said, with that smile she now knew she couldn't trust.

She had never, in all her years painting, believed paint thinner was sexy. Not until Jack stripped her naked, soaked a fluffy washcloth with the stuff and began dabbing it on the paint patches. Of course, his other hand was busy, too, as was his mouth, which may have been how the turpentine came to arouse Laura to a new pitch.

She took her revenge when her turn with the washcloth came, and she didn't declare his body paint-free until he was groaning with the strength of his arousal. He turned the shower on and they stepped under the jets of steaming water, soaping each other and pressing their slick bodies together while they kissed long and deep. She slid her hands over his strong back, taut buttocks, and then took his manhood in one hand, the bar of soap in the other. "I missed a spot," she whispered.

After the shower, he toweled her dripping body with painstaking deliberation. He dried her breasts and then, while he was toweling her belly, leaned forward and sucked her nipples wet just for the pleasure of toweling them again, grinning wickedly when the rough material on her sensitized flesh made Laura gasp. He dried each of her long legs slowly, toweling thoroughly between each of her toes, caressing her until her body felt heavy, liquid. When he hoisted her onto the cool Arborite on the bathroom vanity and parted her thighs, she tipped her head back against the steamy mirror, inhaling the moist air that smelled like citrus shampoo with a hint of paint thinner.

She stopped noticing anything but the feel of his lips once he bent his head and began kissing the flesh of her inner thighs. She whimpered helplessly as he parted the curls that hid her secrets. His tongue touched her, teased her, tormented her until she was sobbing in surrender, her toes curled round his shoulders, her fingers clutching his wet hair.

He dried himself swiftly, then hoisted Laura in his arms and carried her, limp and pampered, to his bed.

His room was furnished simply—a pine chest of drawers and a king-size bed with a pine headboard and a single night table. The walls were white, the curtains and bedspread blue. Everything was neat, orderly, almost impersonal.

A picture of Sara graced the night table, along with a clock radio and a legal thriller. There was a mirror on one wall and a framed picture of Sara and Jack all dressed up, maybe at somebody's wedding. There was no trace of Cory.

He slipped under the sheets beside Laura and she snuggled into him even as she said, "This is a very bad idea. We should get back to work."

"You're right, we should," he said, pulling her on top of him....

HUNGER PANGS WOKE LAURA. She opened her eyes, disoriented and confused. She felt the unfamiliar warmth of a solid body snoring gently behind her, and allowed herself a moment just to savor the experience of waking up with the man she loved.

His arm was draped over her, his hand curled round her breast just as though it belonged there. She glanced at the clock radio. It was after two.

She allowed herself one more minute, just to be. Memorizing the feel of his breath against her hair, the rhythm of his snoring, each warm point where his body touched her own. Letting herself enjoy the exquisite pleasure of knowing that for this one moment in eternity, Jack was hers.

"Jack," she said softly, poking his shoulder.

He muttered and turned over. She allowed herself another moment just to watch him sleeping, filled with such love for this man that her eyes misted. Forcing herself to move, she slipped out of bed and padded to the bathroom to retrieve her paint-crusted clothes. Jack's plaid bathrobe was hanging on a hook on the back of the door.

Bundling her own clothes into a corner, she slipped into his robe. It was soft flannel and smelled of him. She hugged it to her as she padded to the kitchen and began opening cupboards to find the coffee. The intimacy of making coffee in Jack's house, naked but for his bathrobe, had her humming an old love song.

She carried a steaming mug into Jack's room and shook him awake. "Jack, it's two-thirty. Sara will be home soon."

That got his attention. He grumbled like a bear coming out of hibernation, but managed to crawl out of bed and pull fresh underwear, a T-shirt and sweats out of the chest of drawers. Laura watched enviously as he pulled on clean, soft clothes.

"Do you think Sara would suspect anything if I borrowed some clean clothes?" she asked at last.

He turned an amused gaze on her. "If you mean my bathrobe, then, yeah, I think she might suspect something."

"Okay." Laura shrugged, pulling the belt off and letting the robe slide to the floor.

Jack made another of those bear-coming-out-of-hibernation noises and began stalking her. She shrieked and ran round the bed. "Sara's coming."

"A brief reprieve," he promised, turning back to the open drawers and pulling out another T-shirt, and sweatpants with a drawstring waist. Almost as an afterthought he tossed a pair of cotton briefs her way.

It was intimate, and surprisingly erotic, to slip into his underwear.

He watched her with a bemused expression that caused her to drag the outer clothes on fast. Everything was baggy, but the fit wasn't too bad. Even the sweatpants stayed up when Laura pulled the drawstring waist as tight as it would go.

They were sitting at Jack's kitchen table devouring ham sandwiches when Laura remembered Cory and her list of questions. "How did I do on Cory's list?" she asked with a grin.

Jack shook his head sadly. "Not well. She thinks you're a nymphomaniac."

Laura snorted midsandwich. "What do you think?"

He put a hand on her thigh. "I think it's contagious."

Laura stopped chewing as the hand rose higher and

slipped inside the waistband of the sweats. Maybe she *was* a nymphomaniac, she thought, as desire bloomed again in her tired body.

The front door banged and Jack's hand quickly exited her underwear.

"Hi, honey, how was your day?" he called out.

"Wow, Dad, you're home." Sara stepped into the kitchen. "Hi, Laura. How come your hair's wet?"

"Laura had a little accident while she was painting and came here to shower. I lent her some clean clothes."

She had to hand it to Jack. He hadn't lied to his daughter, he'd just skipped all the good parts. He didn't look at her, either, which helped keep her blush to a minimum.

Sara poured a glass of milk and joined them at the table, helping herself to a sandwich. They chatted about her day at school and the progress on the house.

"Why don't you come and help?" Jack asked her. "Laura's a bit behind today since her accident." The six-foot-two, blue-eyed accident.

"Aw, Dad, I can't. Jennifer asked me to her house. We have to study for a math test tomorrow. I only came home to write you a note in case you got home early."

"How about I pick you up at Jennifer's when I finish work, and we'll go for pizza."

"Great. Can Laura come, too?"

His eyes smiled at Laura. "Well, can you?"

She smiled back. "It's a date."

They dropped Sara off at her friend's and headed back to the McNair House.

"I'd better see if the paint's dry in the maid's room

yet," Laura said, forcing herself not to blush, as they entered the old house.

"The hell with the maid's room. Why don't you start on the main rooms down here? I've finished all the messy stuff. I'll just be carving for a while."

She wondered if they'd ever get anything done if they worked within kissing distance of each other. "I don't know..."

He turned a lascivious gaze on her. "I promise not to ravish you outside of lunch and coffee breaks from now on."

Laura felt a warm flush spread through her body at the look in his eyes. She'd spent so much energy making sure they worked as far apart as possible. Now the idea of working together seemed so sensible. She nodded in agreement. "Let me show you my ideas for this room."

She ran out to the van and pulled her design sheets for the entrance hall, parlor and dining room. She had ideas for the remaining rooms on the main floor—the library, morning room and conservatory—but no firm designs yet.

She spread the sheets out for Jack to see, and he held down the rustling paper with one arm, putting the other arm around Laura's waist. "What is this, red? For the living room?" He pointed at her scrawled notes.

"Maroon," she corrected. "Very popular in 1886." He looked so horrified Laura couldn't help but smile. "Don't worry, I'm going to flog the walls."

"Is that how you get them to turn red?" He grinned and her heart flipped.

"Very funny. It's a brushing technique, softens the

color. I'll match the flocked maroon wallpaper I'm using in the dining room."

She pulled away from his arms, putting distance between them when she saw the grin forming on his face. "What are you thinking?"

"I'm thinking how much I like you in red."

At his words, she started reliving what had happened upstairs, in all its glorious details. She looked at Jack sharply, reliving one curious detail.

"Is something wrong?" he asked.

"Do you always carry condoms in your jeans?" She blurted it out before she could stop the words.

Jack looked shocked. "No, of course not."

She stood watching him warily until he smiled, a tender, rueful smile. He put his hands on her shoulders. "I spent all last night planning how I was going to get you in the sack," he admitted.

Happiness spurted through Laura. "You spent all night and came up with crumpled paint sheets for a bed?"

His eyes were twinkling. "Come here."

He took her by the hand and led her up the stairs. She was mystified until they got to the master bedroom. He pulled her through the doorway and left her standing beside the bed while he crossed the room to a paper sack on the floor. It rustled in the silence as he dug into the bag.

"It was your own damned fault for insisting on staying up in the maid's room. Exhibit A." He produced a pair of candles from the bag. "Exhibit B." He waved a bottle of champagne at her. "The ice bucket and ice are in my vehicle, if you care to see them. Exhibit C. Freshly purchased." The box of condoms had ripped cellophane still hanging from it.

Laura bit her lip. "I'm sorry I spoiled your surprise," she said.

"You didn't spoil anything," he said, coming over to slip his arms around her. "It was perfect." He looked at the bed. "Not as comfortable as a freshly made featherbed maybe...but perfect."

Laura leaned into him, inhaling the smell of the laundry soap clinging to his T-shirt, and his own unique musky fragrance. "I'm glad it happened just the way it did. Gran's promised me this bedding for a bridal gift. I'd hate to use it under false pretenses."

Jack let her go then. "Anytime you feel like champagne, just shout." He sounded cheerful enough, but Laura felt him withdraw from her. She wanted to ask him why, but he'd bounded down the stairs, and was pulling his tools together when she reached the main floor.

He kept her entertained all afternoon while they worked in the same room. He was great fun as a working companion, but the intimacy they'd shared was somehow diminished.

9

COLLISEUM PIZZA HADN'T changed its decor since Laura was a little girl. The same dusty, framed pictures of crumbling Roman and Greek landmarks still clung to the stucco walls. Which was why the place was still nicknamed the Roman Ruin. But the pizza was as good as she remembered it, she thought, digging her teeth into yet another lusciously thick slice oozing cheese and sauce.

As ravenously as she ate, she was eating like a bird next to Jack, who chomped down everything in sight. She caught his eye, and he must have read her mind.

"We worked up quite an appetite today," he said innocently enough, but the silent message was clear—it wasn't work, but erotic play that had them pigging out.

While they were eating, a group of boys sauntered in, all black baggy clothes and back-to-front baseball caps. They eyed Sara until she blushed.

"Hey, Sara," one lanky boy said with forced casualness.

"Hey, Ryan." Jack's daughter blushed deeper still as she returned the greeting.

Laura caught the look of irritation on Jack's face and smiled to herself. His nightmare days of fathering a teenage dating daughter were just around the corner.

"Who was that?" he asked, once the boys had left the building.

"Ryan Bailey," Sara mumbled.

"The one who spends half his life in the principal's office." Jack lifted his gaze to the grease-spattered ceiling. "Figures."

Sara rolled her own eyes in a pretty good imitation of her father's disgusted look, and Laura had to choke back a laugh.

She had a feeling there'd be some interesting times ahead.

"Guess what, Daddy? Jennifer's family's going to their cabin at Mount Baker for the weekend. They invited me to go along. Can I? Please?"

"Away for the weekend?" Jack glanced at Laura the same way Ryan Bailey had gazed at Sara. "Sure you can." He seemed to remember his fatherly duty. "If your homework is up to date."

Sara grinned good-naturedly. "It is, Dad. Jennifer's mom's going to phone you and invite me properly."

Laura wondered how often he talked to Sara's friends' moms, playing mother as well as father to his daughter.

Jack reached under the table for her hand and gave it a quick squeeze. She didn't have the heart to tell him she would be in Seattle this weekend checking out horsehair furniture.

When Sara excused herself for the bathroom, Jack turned to Laura. "I am planning to keep you very busy this weekend, Ms. Kinkaide."

"I have to go to Seattle to a furniture auction this weekend." She bit her lip, feeling the same keen disappointment she saw mirrored on Jack's face. Without thinking, without planning to, she blurted, "Why don't you come with me?"

The disappointment was gone in an instant. "I'll bring the champagne."

What was she doing? Laura started panicking. Her apartment was her sanctuary. If Jack invaded that...

And then she glanced up to find him smiling at her in a way that made her toes curl. If her choice was between a weekend alone and an entire weekend with Jack...well, a couple of days with Jack were worth a re-broken heart and a life of misery.

No contest.

JACK ARRIVED FOR WORK in conflicting moods of elation and grumpiness.

"Ja-ack? Can you come up here a minute?" Laura's voice was pitched low, with a suggestion of a waver in the tone. All during his long and very cold shower this morning he'd lectured himself about staying focused on the job today. Hanky-panky in the maid's room, or anywhere else during work hours, was out.

Which made him wonder why he'd stopped to shove a fresh supply of condoms in his pocket.

Just the sound of that low, sultry voice sent all his resolutions flying out of his head, to be replaced by images of Laura, all coy and seductive, waiting for him somewhere upstairs.

As he bolted up the steps, two at a time, visions of what he might find had his libido in overdrive.

He pictured her stretched out on that big old bed in some teensy, black lace, flimsy thing—he didn't care what it was so long as it was crotchless, because right now he didn't think he had the coordination to remove so much as a pair of panties.

Or maybe her voice had come from the maid's room. A new image superimposed itself—Laura in a starched maid's uniform, white cap, apron and silk stockings as black as sin. She'd be in some prim pose with a feather duster—and in seconds he'd have her on her back, her apron flipped over her head while he got very creative with that feather duster.

The stairs echoed beneath his anxious feet as he pounded upward. He paused at the second floor, uncertain whether to go up farther, when he heard his name whispered. It was coming from the bedroom this time.

Damn straight. She'd better get used to the idea of him as the man in her life, in her bed, under her precious antique linens. Otherwise, he might be forced to use those precious antiques to tie her to that nice, sturdy four-poster, while he tortured her with his mouth and hands and every other part of him, until he had her crying out in ecstasy, begging him to be the man in her bed permanently.

He was bursting with anticipation when he tore into the bedroom, hot and hard and ready to plunge into those crotchless panties.

A low, animal growl met his ears and he stopped, just in time, from launching himself onto the bed—on top of an animal that was definitely not Laura.

At first he thought a stray cat had found its way into the house. Then he looked again. Black eyes gleamed at him from behind a telltale black furry mask.

"It's a raccoon!" he cried out in surprise.

"Thank you, Sherlock." Laura stood stock-still on the other side of the bed.

Jack took a step toward the bed, and the raccoon rose to its hind legs and made a sound between a growl and a hiss.

Laura gasped and took a step backward.

He had to admit, he'd seen a lot of raccoons in his time, but this one seemed a little on the ferocious side. It looked like the kind of raccoon that made cats and even small dogs disappear. But it was just a raccoon. Not exactly an exotic creature in the Pacific Northwest.

From the look of Laura, who was in her usual work garb and nothing lacy or crotchless, she hadn't seen a raccoon in a while. Even *he* could smell her fear. "I don't know what to do. Every time I move, it waves its claws at me and hisses." She nearly whimpered.

He decided to punish her, just a little, for the way she'd made him feel yesterday, about not being good enough to share her pristine marriage bed. "I'm sure you'll figure something out."

"Wait!" she squeaked. "You've got to help me."

"Well, I wouldn't want to be accused of any gender biasing. If it was the electrician, Charlie, cornered by a raccoon, or the roofer, Pete, or Lars, the bricklayer, I guess I'd just go back downstairs and get to work." Jack took a step back, toward the door.

The glance she sent him could have melted the North Pole. "Not Charlie, or Pete, or Lars would have done what we did yesterday. And if you ever, ever, want it to happen again, you better do something—"

Her agitated tone must have freaked the raccoon

even more, for it started pacing restlessly, growling low in its throat.

"—now," she whispered in panic.

"Okay. Calm down. I wonder how it got in."

"Who cares? Just make it get out."

"But all the doors were closed and—"

"I don't care if it flew in on a spaceship, make it disappear." Laura was starting to sound as agitated as the raccoon, which wasn't having a beneficial effect on the little guy. He looked like he was about to throw the raccoon version of a hissy fit. Which wouldn't be pretty, considering he was sitting in the middle of Laura's bridal bedding.

"It's just feeling cornered. It's got one of us on either side of it and no escape." Jack spoke in a deliberately slow, soothing voice, hoping to calm at least one of the room's agitated occupants, even if just himself. "I'm going to open the door wide..." He stepped slowly back and pushed the old paneled door all the way open. He made a mental note to put some oil on that squeaking hinge.

"Now I'm going to run downstairs and open the front door. I'll be right back."

"Hurry," Laura whispered.

And he did. He tore downstairs, opened the front door wide and grabbed a broom and shoved on his work gloves. He jogged back up the stairs as quietly as he could and eased himself back into the bedroom, where the scene appeared pretty much the same as before. "Now I'm going to move around the room toward you to give our friend here a clear path out. Here goes."

He moved against the wall and slowly slid around

the room, watched all the way by the raccoon, until he was next to Laura. Jack couldn't resist giving her a reassuring hug around the shoulders, only to have her hug him back fiercely. A rush of protectiveness swamped him. So much for gender bias. If Charlie or Pete ever tried to hug him like that, they'd be eating their teeth for lunch.

"It's not moving."

"Don't worry. I have a backup plan."

"What is it?"

"Run like hell." He squeezed her shoulders again, just to let her know he was joking, and she shot him a withering glance. He eased away from her and pushed the broom forward as he stepped toward the raccoon. It hissed alarmingly. He hoped it wouldn't jump at his face. He had a humane trap at home, but he didn't think Laura was going to think much of the idea of him running home to get it.

"Here goes."

"Be careful."

He turned his head away to protect his face as he gave the raccoon a firm nudge with the broom in the direction of the door. The animal gave a kind of roar and then he heard its claws hitting the floor and running.

There was a shriek from behind him, then Laura hurtled past him and tumbled onto the bed.

He saw a flash of gray and realized the frightened raccoon hadn't run out the door, but under the bed toward them.

Not only did they have sharp little claws and teeth, but some of them carried rabies. Jack jumped up beside

Laura on the bed while the animal regarded them with blatant hostility.

All Jack had accomplished was to reverse their positions. Now they were on the bed, and the raccoon in the spot Laura had just vacated.

"Is there a plan C?" Laura asked.

"Yeah. We shut the little guy in here, go to my house and pick up a live trap. Then we'll let it go out in the woods, somewhere far away."

But just as they eased off the bed, the raccoon made a sudden leap, climbed the new rose tapestry curtains and squeezed out the open window.

"That must be how he got in," he muttered.

Laura got off the bed and went to shut the window, leaving it open just an inch. "And I don't think it's a he."

Jack joined her at the window, just in time to watch the animal leap from the cherry tree into a neighboring fir, where three tiny versions of the same masked face stared out of a nest.

"No wonder she was so upset—she had to get home to her babies."

"The urge to protect those you love is pretty strong," Jack agreed. Something squeezed tight in his chest. Even though there'd been no danger, just the fact that Laura had been nervous had him acting like Sir Galahad. Or maybe one of those fairy-tale guys fighting dragons to win princesses. Of course, he wasn't much of a prince. But then, one frantic mother raccoon wasn't much of a dragon, either.

"Jack..." Her soft voice in his ear pulled him out of his reverie.

"Mmm?"

"Ah, just this once, I'm glad you were gender-biased."

He gazed down into those gorgeous, rich brown eyes staring back at him, and all his earlier fantasies came rushing back.

He turned her so her back was to the window, and trapped her with his arms. "That's good. Because I'm going to bias your gender again," he whispered, low and menacing.

He felt the quiver of response.

"I'm going to bias your gender until you beg for mercy."

"I won't," she replied, deliberately sultry.

"You will," he promised, and shut her up by kissing her.

Her lips were soft and full and they trembled slightly beneath his. *Poor kid, she really had been scared.* He pulled her in tighter and a little sigh escaped. Her lips opened to him and his greedy tongue plunged inside, savoring the hot wet depth of her mouth.

Her trembling was getting worse, not better, the more they kissed. He realized, with a little masculine thrill, that *he* was making her tremble. Her tongue stroked his and in seconds he was back in a state of raging arousal, even worse than when he'd first burst into the room.

His hands groped for the snaps on her overalls, but she wasn't the only one trembling. He fumbled, trying to pop the ridiculously small metal disks, drawing back from her mouth to pant, "From now on, you wear skirts to work."

"Skirts..." Her eyes were unfocused, her lips passion-plump. He felt her fingers cup his arousal and rub him through his jeans.

He groaned, enjoying the delicious torture. He was going to explode any second. Reluctantly, he pulled her hands away. "Do you own any crotchless panties?"

"No." She undid his belt.

"I'll buy you some."

He had the bib down and her T-shirt up and over her head.

"What color?" She leaned against the window. Dappled sunlight haloed her and left her face shadowed. He hoped to hell the just-blossoming cherry tree would hide them from view.

"Black. Red. Pink..." *Who cared what color?* "A pair for every day of the year."

Her breasts were creamy-golden; the darker tips puckered and rose the minute he touched them, just brushing his palms over the tight peaks. She arched toward him and a shaft of morning sun played across her chest, turning the tips to russet.

He lowered his head reverently and sucked a nipple into his mouth.

A shudder ran through her body.

For a long time he licked and sucked, just the nipple, then trailed a wet path to the other side and repeated the process. When he lifted his head, the tips glistened, diamondlike against the soft creamy velvet of her skin.

The denim overalls sagged at her hips, the bib flipped over the greatest of her treasures. He kissed a path down her belly, leaving a trail of goose bumps, before he eased the overalls and her panties down in one push.

Then he settled her hips on the wide windowsill, parted her knees and knelt before her.

A soft breeze from the open window wafted over them, bringing the scent of cherry blossoms, as he kissed his way up her thigh, forcing himself to go slow, yet burning with the need to taste her.

When at last he parted the glistening curls and lapped the salt honey of her, she cried out and grabbed on to the heavy curtains. He savored the wet, quivering feminine flesh, taking his time, loving the little panting noises she made, the mindless way she pumped her hips beneath his tongue.

"Please...please..." she sobbed. He was too much of a gentlemen to ever bring it up, but he treasured the knowledge that he'd just made her beg. As he'd promised he would.

He had his jeans down and the condom on in record time, needing to be inside her as much as he knew she needed him. Moving between her spread legs, he grasped her hips, hard enough to hold her still beneath him, and gave her what she begged for.

He thrust deep and hard, all the way in.

She shattered as he entered that tight slick passage, her hips jerking right up off the windowsill to meet his as she wrapped her legs round him. She clung to the curtains fisted in her hands while he supported her hips and rode the climax with her.

He kissed and soothed her for a minute, letting her get her breath back, then he got to work stoking her up once more.

"Again," he whispered.

"I can't," she panted. But the quivering flesh clenched tight around him and he didn't believe her.

He increased the tempo, wanting to give her everything he had. She was hot, tight—and the way she was moving, she was going to make a liar out of herself, which she did, crying out a second time, and this time he exploded, right along with her.

"I can't believe it. I never come twice," she murmured a few moments later.

"You're in the hands of a superior lover, Ms. Kinkaide," he joked. But her words thrilled him to the core. He wanted to reach her in ways no man ever had, or could.

She chuckled and slumped against him.

It wasn't exactly comfortable, the pair of them heaped on the floor. He eyed the big bed, hulking in the middle of the room—big enough for a sexual gymnasium. If it was the last thing he ever did, he was going to get Laura Kinkaide naked in that bed.

"Come on." He pulled her to her feet and tried to drag her toward the bed, but he'd forgotten they both had their pants around their ankles. She giggled as they stumbled, clinging together to keep from falling. "Round two."

"You're ready to do it again?" Her eyes opened wide.

"I told you. I'm a superior lover. Anyway, your sexy body is enough to recharge any man." He started hopping toward the bed.

She pulled away, breathless and laughing. "We can't, Jack. It's Wednesday."

"In case you hadn't noticed, I do my best gender biasing on Wednesdays." He lifted her hair and put his tongue right on that magic spot beneath her ear, the quickest way he knew past her defenses.

She let out a frustrated groan. "No, no. The committee meeting's tonight. I have to finish some things."

Damn. He wanted to get the rest of the carving done on the downstairs mantel before the committee trouped in. He pulled up his pants. The bed would have to wait.

He watched her pull her clothes back on, and was shocked at how much he wanted to take her all over again.

"Back to business," she said, snapping her overall bib on crooked.

"Just don't forget you've got some very unfinished business—with me."

"I CALL THIS MEETING to order," Delores Walters announced firmly, silencing the excited buzz of a dozen voices gathered in Laroche's high school.

"Unlike most committees I've served on over the years, the Save the McNair Committee has actually accomplished what it set out to do." She paused for the smattering of laughter. "And remarkably efficiently, I might add. We'll hear from the two primary contractors later, and then we'll tour the property."

Jack's eyelids were getting heavy, just as they always did when he had to attend a meeting like this. He knew it was important to pay attention, and he really tried.

He'd downed two cups of coffee during the milling-around time before the business started. But committee meetings were like sleeping pills—something caffeine alone couldn't combat.

He sat at the back of the classroom where the meeting

was being held. Classrooms just naturally made him drift to the back. Laura, he noted, was sitting at the front. Typical suck-up-to-the-teacher behavior.

He let his head loll against the back wall, trying to appear riveted by the proceedings, and stifled a yawn. The business went from previous minutes through donations to financial position.

There were the usual droning voices, the usual questions and comments from the ones who just couldn't sit still in a group without saying something. He knew them all, of course. The committee treasurer was Mary, his bank manager, who was a lot less friendly since Cory had grilled her about her sex life. In her measured voice she recounted the financial position.

Jack liked Mary. He liked the calm way she spoke about things without rambling off the point. He had a pretty good head for numbers himself, so he listened to Mary's report, putting together a mental picture of the project's finances. His head jerked back as he pieced the truth together from her summary of debits and credits. Suddenly, he didn't feel sleepy anymore.

A government grant they had preliminary approval on had just been canceled. Mary read from an official-looking letter. Fiscal belt-tightening, it explained, meant that money for education and health care had to come before heritage projects. Perhaps in a year or two...

In her calm, banker's way, Mary was telling them there wasn't enough money to complete the work on McNair House. Instinctively, he glanced to the front row and noticed that Laura's back was unnaturally straight.

As though she felt him staring at her, she turned and

gazed directly at him, a question in her eyes, concern in her creased forehead.

He nodded, and Mary's next words confirmed his conclusions.

"I'm afraid, ladies and gentlemen, that unless a miracle occurs, this committee will run out of money before the renovations are complete."

There was a collective holding of breath as the dozen or so committee members got the point. Then hands were thrust in the air, waving madly.

Two hours later the group was as far from solving their financial difficulties as when Mary had first informed them of the crisis.

"I suggest we get on with the tour, anyway," said Mrs. Walters, in her brisk way. If there was a way to save the project, Jack knew she'd find it.

The school was a scant block away from the McNair House, so the meeting moved en masse and on foot to view the renovation-in-progress.

Jack clomped along with the rest of the dejected, and much quieter, group, sensing when Laura fell into step beside him. He let his gaze focus on the house standing high and proud on the hill.

It had seen so much, that house; weathered natural storms, financial disasters, emotional upheavals. Just when it was getting a second glorious chance at life, another financial disaster had hit.

Which put Jack out of a job. Not that he was short of work; he had a list of projects waiting. It was more that he hated unfinished business. And besides, this job had become personal.

He did some quick mental arithmetic. If he donated

all his time, that would cut the shortfall considerably. He could then use his own donation to guilt some of his suppliers into donating materials—especially if they got some kind of recognition from the city for their philanthropy. He could persuade them that being generous corporate citizens also made good business sense.

Beside him Laura spoke.

He was so caught up in his idea he had to ask her to repeat herself.

"I said, how's your financial position?"

He looked at her blankly, knowing that part of the reason he was suddenly so interested in saving a civic monument had to do with Laura. He wasn't ready to give up the job that kept her working by his side every day.

"I'm thinking about donating my time." She said it rapidly, sounding nervous. "But I can afford to do it. I mean, my company can. In fact, I could use the charitable donation to help with my taxes. What I was thinking is that we'd both say we were donating half our time. I'll make up the difference."

Irritation stabbed at Jack. Did she think he was some kind of deadbeat? Maybe he wasn't a flashy guy like her swanky city friends, but his finances were more than respectable. He certainly didn't need any handouts. *He* planned on dishing out the charity.

The grudge he was carrying around was getting pretty heavy. He was still smarting from finding out he was good enough for a lusty romp in the servants' quarters, but not worthy to dirty Miss Kinkaide's pristine bridal sheets.

"That's very generous of you." He tried to keep the

irritation from his voice. "I was thinking about donating my time, as well. I can afford it, too, as a matter of fact."

Wanting to rub her nose in the memory of their earlier coupling, he leaned closer. "I guess we owe the old girl something."

She glanced up at him, and he watched her teeth start gnawing on her plump lower lip. It filled him with an urge to do the job for her. From her lip, his teeth would travel to the sensitive lobe of her ear and do a little more gentle gnawing. And he wouldn't stop there. When he thought of all the places on that sweet body he'd like to put his mouth, he felt himself harden. Which wasn't the greatest idea, considering he was halfway up Main Street in the middle of a committee meeting.

"Are you sure?" she whispered uncertainly.

"Absolutely." He smiled down at her and tried to get his mind back on track.

The tour was a dismal affair. Jack watched the committee members sigh sadly over the new work, alternately admiring it and commiserating that it would never be shared with the rest of the community and tourists. He wished Gran McMurtry were here instead of home nursing a sore throat. She would soon smarten them up.

Finally, when the glum dozen reassembled in the cavernous drawing room, Jack leaned forward and put his lips to Laura's ear. "Can we tell them now?"

He felt her involuntary shudder as his breath wafted by that spot, just below her earlobe. If they were alone...

But they weren't.

She turned to peer into his eyes, her forehead creased

with uncertainty. "Are you sure you can afford this? It's not some macho thing, is it?"

"Are you sure *you* can afford this?" he whispered back.

She smiled and nodded. "You tell them."

He gazed at her searchingly a moment longer, then turned to face the group. "Before you go, folks, Laura and I have an announcement."

"Oh, I knew it." The sensible Mrs. Walters was wreathed in smiles, her plain face flushed pink. "I couldn't be happier."

How on earth could she know? Jack looked over at Laura, who raised her eyebrows. He turned back to the group. "Laura and I have decided to donate our time on the McNair House."

For some reason Mrs. Walters looked disappointed.

Mary stepped forward, her face the friendliest Jack had seen it since the night of Chip's party. She was beaming.

"That's wonderful news. I'll have to run the numbers, but I believe our budget can cover the cost of supplies to finish the project, so long as we stick to essentials."

After the last thank-yous and compliments on the fine work had been expressed, Laura and Jack were left to lock up the house.

Laura had been quiet during the final part of the tour. He walked over to where she leaned against the banister, and put one arm around her, tilting her face with his free hand. "Regretting your generosity?"

She shook her head. Her eyes seemed to catch light from somewhere and glowed like the richest mahogany. "I'm regretting our weekend in Seattle." She moved her arms up around his neck.

His body stirred in response. Just being near her was the biggest turn-on. "What's to regret?"

"I hardly think Mary would call a horsehair set essential. I'm afraid we'll have to skip the auction." She bit her lip, just like she always did when she was thinking hard.

Disappointment hit Jack like a blow. He'd been looking forward to the weekend so keenly it was making him nervous. He couldn't afford to fall in love with a woman he couldn't have permanently. Of course, he had to face the possibility it was already too late. Maybe he was already in love with Laura.

"What is it? Why are you looking at me like that?" Laura asked him. From this close he could see the dents her teeth had made in her lip. He leaned down to kiss them away, and she leaned forward to meet him halfway.

He kissed the dents away. He did such a thorough job Laura's lips were passion-swollen, her eyes blazing with urgent desire, when he lifted his head at last.

The same desire burned in him, stronger than anything he'd ever known. He wanted to throw her to the ground and take her savagely, there on the floor. He felt a primitive need to stamp his ownership all over her body—mark her as his territory.

He was no Lady Chatterley's lover, to be banished back to his gardener's hut when my lady was done with him. He, Jack, wanted to be master. Free to take her anywhere in the damn house he pleased. He wanted to drive himself deep inside her body, plant his seed inside her. Let all men know she was his. And most of all, make sure *she* understood she was his.

Her eyes were dark, black almost, drawing him into her. He heard his own growl, deep and low as he claimed her mouth again, telling her with his lips, his tongue, his hands, that she was his.

Reaching out, he flicked the light switch off, plunging the hallway into darkness but for the glow of moonlight stealing through the leaded windows.

She whimpered as darkness cloaked them, her hands grabbing, grasping him everywhere, pulling him against her with a wild abandon that sent his own urgency skyrocketing.

He dragged his jacket off, threw it on the floor. Hers followed. They tore at resisting buttons, stubborn zippers, yanked and tossed clothing anywhere in their blinding need to be naked and together.

Panting, wordless, they fell on the piled clothing, where she wrapped her legs around him and drew him into her.

He thrust deep and hard as though he could push through and into her very soul. She cried out, arching up to him, head thrown back, her body sucking him greedily into her depths.

They rolled and she was astride him, her naked body gilded by moonlight so she resembled some ancient goddess come to sport with her mortal lover. She was wild, untamable, gripping his shoulders fiercely as she rode him.

Panting, he matched her rhythm, driving up and up to some impossible pinnacle.

A cry spilled out from deep in her throat, and her

head tipped back even as her body began bucking wildly with the spasms that shook her.

Her violent climax was too much for his self-control. He rocketed over the edge, right along with her, and shot straight to the stars.

With a soft moan, she collapsed on top of him and he held her gently, listening to the sobbing pants in his ear. Her lips pressed to his neck, trembling with reaction.

He felt such tenderness for this woman wrapped in his arms that his own hands trembled against her tousled hair and he smiled at his foolishness.

Where he'd tried to proclaim mastery, he'd become more enslaved.

"I'm freezing," she said, when they could finally talk again. Jack rose, reluctantly, but had to agree it was too cold for lazing around enjoying the afterglow. They ferreted through the darkness, for some reason loath to put on the lights.

"How did your sock end up halfway up the stairs?" she demanded, half-naked since she couldn't find her bra.

"Is this what you're looking for?" Jack fished a tail of satin and lace out of the fireplace.

It was when he pulled on his jeans that it hit him. "Oh, my God. I didn't use anything." He slumped on the stairs as the awful realization struck a body blow. How could he have been so careless? He heard the horror he felt reflected in his voice.

"Laura, I'm sorry," he rasped.

It couldn't be happening, not again. Hadn't he learned all about birth control the hard way? He rubbed his forehead as though he could wipe away the stunned feeling that gripped him. "I, um...are you on anything?"

"No." She spoke quietly, without anger.

"I can't believe I was so stupid!" His rage was sudden and furious. He was plunged back in time to the awful days and weeks after he and Cory had made the same mistake.

His ex-wife had been trapped and bitter, throwing furious accusations in his face every chance she got. She blamed him for ruining her life, as though he'd slipped up deliberately. He'd tried to be sympathetic, but late at night he'd sneak down to the high school football field and just sit on the bench for hours, knowing he'd lost his dream, as well.

Jack had spent years atoning for his mistake. In the past weeks since Laura had come back into his life he'd felt he was getting another chance. A chance to get it right. And here was history repeating itself again. If Laura turned on him he wouldn't blame her. But deep down a seed of hope began to grow. What if he'd given her a child? She'd have to be a permanent part of his life then.

"You're sorry?" Her voice echoed strangely in the dark hallway.

There was a long silence. He didn't know what to say.

"I'm a grown woman, Jack. I take part of the responsibility, too." Laura's voice grated. She sounded mad. She didn't want his baby. What had he expected?

A huge chasm seemed to open between them in the time it took Laura to button her shirt and Jack to find his other sock. When he put his coat back on, the faint scent of Laura clung to it. He pulled it close around him. He wanted to take her in his arms, but she had a force field of anger around her that prevented him coming near.

"Laura, I don't want to leave it like this. Please—"

She swung on him. "Leave what? There's nothing to talk about."

"But what if you're pregnant?" He'd been down this road before. He remembered the anger, the recriminations, the tears. The lousy five-year penance marriage. He wanted it to be different with Laura, but he could see history repeating itself, right before his burning eyes.

"Haven't you ever heard of the morning-after pill? If you slip up and take this pill soon enough after, it prevents pregnancy." He didn't have to see her face; he could feel her anger.

His own anger spurted. He felt like she was sloughing him off along with his unwanted sperm. "How do you know?"

The temperature was rising rapidly in the cold hall. "I've read about it. I've never had to use it before," she spat. "My boyfriends are usually more careful. In your case, I should have been prepared."

Ouch. That hurt. The recriminations were starting already, along with this sick feeling in his gut. He thought getting Cory pregnant had screwed up his life, but in a flash he knew that earlier experience was nothing compared to losing Laura. And he was losing her. He didn't know what to say to stop her from walking out that door.

It was open. Cool air washed over him. He saw Laura silhouetted in the doorway. He had to stop her.

"Wait, Laura, please—"

The door shut quietly in his face.

10

TEARS RAN UNHEEDED down Laura's cheeks as she sat on the deserted beach. The rising wind smacked her wet face, its salt-tangy mist stinging her nostrils with every sobbing breath.

A dark cloud mass rolled across the night sky, snuffing stars as it closed in. Good. Nothing should sparkle tonight.

She sat on a damp log and listened to the waves thudding angrily against the rocky beach. In the Stupidest Days of her Life category, today was right up there. She had just had unprotected sex for the first time ever, and with a guy whose life had already been derailed once because of it. She banged her heels against the pitted log. *Stupid, stupid, stupid.*

She knew why she'd let it happen.

She loved Jack.

She had told him so with her body tonight, holding nothing back during their lovemaking. His body had responded with the same message—she was sure of it.

Even in the amazing vortex of their passion, Laura had been well aware there was nothing between them.

It hadn't mattered. In fact, it added to the excitement. She hadn't wanted any barrier between them. She was twenty-eight. Old enough to know what she wanted. Stupidly, she'd thought he felt the same way.

She wanted Jack. She wanted children, too. Jack's children. Those chubby, rose-cheeked cherubs of her childhood fantasy. Except it wasn't a fantasy anymore. She wanted the real children. The ones who would keep her up at night when they were sick, who would bring home their skinned knees and dirty faces. Date kids their father didn't approve of.

She even wanted the real Jack, the man who snored in his sleep, who got jealous when a guy like Chip came on to her—and who held his pride around him like a shield, pretending he was strong and tough even when he was hurting and vulnerable. She choked on a sob and tasted cold rainwater and warm tears.

She had found the man who could get past her fear of intimacy. She would still love Jack if he bit his nails.

And he'd just made it brutally clear he didn't want her or another child. She wrapped her arms around her middle and rocked against the pain.

In the distance, lightning forked tongues of fire in the black sky. *One Mississippi, two Mississippi...* She counted the time between lightning flash and thunder without even thinking. *Eleven Mississippi*, and the boom she'd expected still made her jump. The storm was eleven miles away, according to her scientific reckoning. Close enough.

What had made her say that to Jack about the morning-after pill? She'd seen a poster about it in her doctor's waiting room once, but she wouldn't take a pill to erase what had happened tonight. It was such a long shot, anyway. Laura was toward the end of her cycle and really doubted a pregnancy would result from tonight's escapade.

But if it did, that was fine with her. If she were going to have a child she'd choose Jack for the father any day. Even if he didn't come as part of the package. In twelve years Laura had never found anyone who appealed to her like Jack did. If she left the island with his child inside her, at least she'd have something.

Laura's wind-whipped face felt raw. The storm was closing in. Five Mississippi—no, six.

As she slipped off the log and eased away the damp denim plastered to her thighs, she was certain of one thing. Even if she had his child, she wouldn't take Jack just because he felt guilty. She was an emotionally stable and financially secure adult, not a frightened teenager. She was perfectly prepared to bring up a child on her own. She needed no guilty husband.

WHEN SHE FINALLY returned home, Gran was upstairs in her room with the light out, presumably asleep; at least Laura was spared having to face those shrewd eyes. She crawled into bed exhausted and cold, but calm. The storm outside was getting closer, but Laura's emotional storm had spent itself. She hugged her arms around her belly and closed her eyes.

Sleep was almost upon her when she realized she hadn't thought once this evening about running back to Seattle. As painful as the process was, she had a feeling she'd finally grown up.

It looked like Jack and she were history...again, but Laura knew she would finish the house. She remembered the pain in Jack's voice when he'd called out to her as she was leaving. He must be terrified she was going to make a lot of demands on him. Well, she wasn't.

She would sit him down calmly and let him know he was off the hook. For his sake she would make sure he didn't see how she was hurting inside. Then she would finish the job she'd come to Laroche to do and finally take her rebroken heart away with her.

And if she was very lucky she would have a precious reminder of the man she would always love growing deep inside her body.

LAURA WOKE WITH A START, uncertain for the moment why. Then her dark room lit up as lightning flashed. Almost immediately thunder boomed. She winced at the sound and squinted to where her beside clock glowed 2:13 a.m. Laura groaned and shoved the pillow over her head to block out the storm, when a new sound broke in on her consciousness.

A siren wailed in the night.

In Seattle, the sound was common, but here in Laroche, where there was a total of one ambulance, one fire engine and two police cars, it was rare indeed.

Laura threw back the covers, padded to the window and stared out into the stormy night. A stand of cedars whipped their ragged arms in a wild dance.

The siren stopped its insistent wail, but Laura couldn't see any action anywhere. Why did she feel so uneasy? Another bolt of lightning shot out of the angry sky, and there was a pause of a few seconds before the thunder caught up.

Laura couldn't shake her instinct that something was wrong. Knowing sleep was beyond her, she didn't bother climbing back into the rumpled bed. Instead she swiftly dressed in jeans and a sweater and crept down-stairs.

She needed to check on the McNair House.

She grabbed a coat, stepped into a pair of Grandpa's old rubber boots and slipped quietly out the back door. As she strode up the hill, fat drops of rain fell. The air still felt charged and turbulent even though the storm was dying down to a distant rumble. Above the sound of the rain she heard her own panting as she quickened her pace.

She saw the fire truck first.

She'd turned the corner onto Main Street, her eyes burning as they tried to penetrate the darkness. The truck's red lights flashed rhythmically right outside the McNair House.

"No," Laura whimpered, running forward.

It was like being caught in a nightmare. The faster she ran in the clumsy rubber boots, the farther away her destination seemed. From this angle, the house looked fine. But the red flashing light warned her of disaster.

It was only when she got past the fire engine that she saw the trunk of the giant old cherry tree split like a twig, its charred edges steaming beneath the rain.

She remembered leaning out, trying to reach that same majestic old tree from the bedroom window when Jack had taped off the downstairs. Now the tree was reaching into the bedroom window. When it had fallen, it had taken a huge bite out of the roof.

Her house, her precious house, was as damaged as her heart. The back of her throat ached. She wanted to cry, but her well of tears seemed to have run dry.

She watched a firefighter hose the tree, the roof, the

carefully decorated interior of the master bedroom, with great gushes of water. All Laura could think of was the hours she'd spent on those damned cabbage roses.

"'Scuse me, ma'am, you'll have to stand over there." A firefighter pointed across the street. He glimpsed her face and his voice softened. "Don't you worry. The fire's out now. It's all over."

She nodded. But she knew from experience that putting out a fire caused as much damage as the fire itself. She moved on leaden feet to the other side of the road, where half a dozen people stood around watching and murmuring.

Jack was there, watching not the busy firefighters, but her. She walked toward him. Couldn't seem to stop her feet from moving in his direction. She didn't say anything, just stood beside him while rain pelted them. No one seemed to have an umbrella.

After a minute he put an arm round her, and she was too unhappy to protest. She stood and watched water drip down the side of the old house like tears. The sky joined in earnest then, and she could hardly see for the downpour.

Jack pulled his collar up over his neck, squinting as he gazed into the pelting rain. "As soon as they'll let me, I'll put a tarp over the hole. Stop the rain getting in."

"What's the point?"

He looked at her sharply. "I'll feel like I at least tried to save her."

Laura shrugged and moved away. Then walked back. "Can I come with you?"

He shook his head. "They're only letting me in because I'm trained as a volunteer firefighter."

"Can you try and save the bedding?"

She remembered her grandmother's precious quilt and her own foolish hopes. A lump rose in her throat.

He nodded.

She turned away and strode off through the rain, past the rumbling fire truck, unable to watch any longer. Unable to stand so near to Jack and not beg him to love her as much as she loved him.

It was over.

It was all over.

LAURA WOKE the next morning with a headache, swollen eyes and chapped skin.

She dabbed cold water on her eyes, covered the chapped skin with moisturizer and foundation, and put on makeup to hide the ravages her emotions and the elements had inflicted. She swallowed a painkiller for her aching head and wished they made one for heartache. Extra strength.

When she got downstairs, Gran took one look at her and held her arms wide. Laura ran into them just as she always had from the time she was a little girl. The two hugged quietly for a long time.

"I'm so sorry, honey," Gran said. "Thanks for remembering the bedding. Jack brought it over early this morning. It's a little damp in places, but it'll be fine. I should never have sent it up there in the first place. Sentimental old fool."

Laura felt her grandmother shaking in her arms. She couldn't be crying. Gran never cried. But a sniffle gave her away. A rush of feeling for this woman caught Laura and she hugged her fiercely, barely managing to hold back her own tears.

"I'm sorry, too, Gran. I really loved that old place. Don't cry."

"I'm not crying, it's just this darned cold," her grandmother sniffled. "Jack asked that you call him this morning."

Laura turned away and went to pour coffee, busying herself with milk and sugar to avoid the old woman's eyes.

"He said it was important."

"I don't think it's about the house." Laura sighed. Better to get this over with. "We had a fight last night." She stirred the dark liquid intently, watching the spoon circle round and round the pottery mug. "I guess you know we've been...I...." Her voice petered out. She put the coffee on the counter, untouched, and wiped streaming eyes with the back of her hand.

This time it was Gran who did the hugging. "So much disaster in one night," the old woman mused. "Are you going to call him?"

Laura shook her head, sniffing. "It's over, Gran."

"Maybe he'll call back."

THE BIG OLD GRANDFATHER clock had just struck noon, and Laura was sitting, dazed, staring out the window at the rain.

Disaster on all fronts.

She had done the one thing she'd promised herself she would not do. She had fallen in love with Jack all over again.

Or had she ever stopped?

She'd loved him since she was sixteen years old. She would always love him. She accepted that no man would ever take his place in her heart; he was the missing part of herself and, even if she never saw him again, which would be wise, he would always be a part of her.

Somehow, the old McNair House had got all tangled up in her feelings about Jack. And now even that was a disaster. She had so many dreams invested in that house. She wondered what would happen to it. Perhaps it would be kinder to pull the poor thing down and be done with it. Put up condos or a supermarket.

When the phone on the table rang, Laura answered, her tone husky.

"Isn't it terrible about the house?" Mrs. Walters sounded truly distressed. "We're getting the committee together today to try and decide what's best. But, of course, we'll have to ask you to stop work for now."

"Of course. I understand."

"I'm so sorry, dear."

"Me, too."

"Would you tell your grandmother the meeting's scheduled for two o'clock today in the mayor's chambers?"

JACK CALLED HIS BUDDY NED of Ned's Tree Topping to get the damaged tree out of the bedroom window. He had no authorization from the committee, and frankly didn't care. If the cost ended up coming out of his own pocket, so be it. He had the strangest sense of urgency about the house.

He needed to save it.

It was pretty obvious the place wasn't going to be any tourist attraction come summer, and he had a strong hunch his contract was about to end. But Jack wanted to protect the old girl from further damage.

While Ned and his crew heaved and hacked the tree out of the window and into firewood, Jack tacked heavy plastic sheeting over the gaping hole in the roof and window.

Inside, he set up a couple of industrial drying fans he'd rented that morning, along with a portable emergency generator. With the fans roaring full blast, connected to the chugging generator, he paused to look around.

The damage wasn't too bad, all things considered. Enough neighbors had seen and heard the lightning strike that the fire department had caught the blaze almost as soon as it started. The water damage was more serious, but he was sure the whole project could be salvaged if there was only more money. He adjusted the roaring dryers slightly and then began a more thorough inspection.

He agreed with the fire crew's initial assessment that structurally the damage was minimal. He felt perfectly safe wandering the rooms, although he wore his hard hat just in case. Lightning was funny. It traveled in uncanny ways, and the worst devastation was sometimes concealed.

Jack tried to work out the exact path the lightning had taken so he could uncover any hidden disaster areas. He got his notebook out and jotted down his findings, took a few measurements. He could put a rough estimate together of what it would cost to repair the damage.

It was probably hopeless, but he had to try. Keeping busy also kept his mind off the lead weight that had established residence in his stomach since Laura had taken off on him the previous night.

He'd called her first thing in the morning, left his cell number so she could reach him wherever he was. But she hadn't called. Twice he'd started to punch in Gran's number, but each time he stopped, afraid of where Laura might be. As the morning crawled by he envisioned her at some clinic, popping the magic morning-after pill.

The rational part of his brain recognized that that was the sensible thing to do. But it made him feel like his love was no more to Laura than an inconvenience, easily remedied with a pill or two.

He was pacing restlessly, open notebook in his hand, when he stumbled. "What the..." He looked down in startled surprise and noticed a couple of floorboards jutting up. It struck him as odd that the floor would have buckled just here.

He knelt, puzzled, and wiggled a board. He was even more surprised when the fir plank popped out smoothly in his hands. The edges weren't jagged, but sawn straight across.

Surprise turned to excitement as he peered down into the dark hole under the floor, thinking of hidden treasure. He lowered himself to the ground and thrust his arm into the recess until his reaching fingers touched something hard. A prickle of anticipation ran up his spine as he pulled out a cloth-wrapped object.

He felt like Indiana Jones as he hunkered down on the floor and carefully opened the cloth. Inside was no crusty treasure chest containing a fortune in jewels. The item in his hands was a plain black, leather-bound book.

As he eased open the age-worn cover, a musty smell hit him. The handwriting on the flyleaf was faded, but legible, with lots of old-fashioned curlicues. "Elizabeth McNair, 1886."

A diary. *Wow,* he thought, *wait till Laura sees this.*

The rounded, flowing writing drew him into the world of Elizabeth McNair and Laroche more than a century ago. The old paper crackled as he carefully turned the page and read the first entry.

I begin this journal as a record of my new life as the wife of my beloved Albert. I am conscious of a powerful notion that such a love ought to be recorded, which I shall try to do within these pages. I feel new life stirring in me and one day I hope my children and their children will read these pages and know that their beginnings were happy ones.

I chose today to begin my journal because our house is almost ready. Such excitement I feel, and pride in my Albert, who has built me this splendid home. He had the stonemason carve The House of Love into a large granite boulder, which Albert swore he planned to have set in the gateway for all to see. Of course, I laughed at such nonsense, but am secretly much pleased. He used the stone instead as the cornerstone of the foundation. It is hidden from all eyes, but is our secret, and it gives me much joy.

Goose bumps rose on Jack's arms.

He held the book reverently in his hands. So Laura had been right all along. Her voice echoed back to him from childhood. "This house was built with love, Jack, can't you feel it?"

Love. The cornerstone of a house. It was a crazy idea. Crazier still that a teenager could feel that love a century later.

He flipped ahead a few pages.

Nearly lost Cook again last night after she came face-to-face with a bear on her visit to the necessary. She is such a good cook, I do wish she could accustom herself to this new land, but I fear one day she will head back to Boston in spite of all our pleas and the monstrous salary Albert pays her.

Jack propped himself more comfortably in a corner and read on. He learned about the early days of Laroche firsthand. He also learned how to make rosehip jelly and how to preserve local fruits and berries for winter.

He learned a few secrets about Albert and Elizabeth's private life that made him feel like a Peeping Tom. And he experienced with Elizabeth McNair her pangs of childbirth, until he was shifting restlessly on the hard, damp floor, his own gut hurting.

He looked up at last from the book, which hardly filled his big hands, and sensed the spirit of Elizabeth and Albert in the house. He had a spooky feeling that they had passed their special home to two people further on in time who felt as they did.

Laura and him and the house. They went together.

What was he thinking? The house was a ruin. The idea was crazy. *He* was crazy.

He rubbed the cracked leather cover of the diary in his hands. He wasn't a guy who believed in signs, or ghosts, or messages from other worlds, but as he held that book, he knew what he had to do. He had to get this house for Laura, and her child, if she was carrying one.

Maybe he could show her, as Albert had shown his Elizabeth, how much he cared. Maybe then she would forgive him, in time learn to love him. He had to try, because he felt part of him had come to life while Laura was back here on the island, but it would die again if she left.

IT FELT LIKE SOMEONE had died. Laura wandered Gran's house, not knowing what to do with herself. Any activity seemed disrespectful, somehow.

She drove Gran to the meeting at city hall. "Are you sure you're well enough to go out?"

"Of course. It's just a silly cold. You'd better drive me by the house first. I suppose I should inspect the damage, though Lord knows, I don't want to."

Laura didn't want to, either, but she helped Gran descend from her van and walk to the edge of the taped-off area to look at the damage in full daylight.

The tree was gone, cut down to a scarred black stump, and clear plastic now covered the missing chunk of roof and wall. Still, the blackened hole looked like a bomb had ripped through it. Bright yellow electric cords snaked down the side of the house and round the corner to where a generator rumbled. Again she wondered, *What's the point?*

While her grandmother was at the meeting, Laura pottered around the kitchen, making quiche and salad. She should have been packing, but didn't have the heart for it. How could she leave so much unfinished business?

She wondered if she'd meet up with Jack again. He hadn't made any attempt to see her today, apart from the feeble message that she should call him. Maybe it was just as well. All her foolish dreams were over. The sooner she accepted that and got on with her life the better.

She heard a car stop outside and her hands flew to her face. *Jack.* She ran upstairs to put on fresh lipstick and run a comb through her hair. Her heart hammered.

Then she heard voices downstairs and realized it was Gran and Mrs. Walters, back from the meeting. Laura trod downstairs to the kitchen a lot more slowly than she'd pounded up the same stairs moments before. "I thought you were going to phone me. I would have picked you up."

"It was no trouble, Laura," the committee chairwoman answered. "Your gran and I wanted a few minutes to chat, anyway, away from all the fidgets."

Laura smiled at Mrs. Walters's term for the other committee members. "Do you want some tea or coffee?" she asked politely.

"Get the whiskey, dear," Gran said, sitting down heavily in her chair. "We all need it."

They sat over their drinks at the oak kitchen table while Mrs. Walters confirmed the worst. The new damage had knocked the heart out of the committee. There wasn't enough money, or time, to complete the house before the tourist season began.

"I'm so sorry, Laura," Mrs. Walters said. "The city's lawyer will contact you about some kind of severance, since your contract has been canceled."

"I'm just sorry for the house," Laura said.

"I can't bear to see that lovely old home turned into condos," Mrs. Walters wailed. "After all our hard work. The developer isn't even an islander. He must have an inside source of information, though, because he's made another offer for the property—much lower, of course, now he knows about the damage. The offer expires next Friday."

"But that's only a week from now. The city doesn't have to accept the offer, surely?"

"It's the only offer that's been made on that property in thirty years. Unless another one comes in before Friday, McNair house will be bulldozed." Mrs. Walters' voice wavered and she hid her emotions in a deep swallow of whiskey.

The committee chairwoman finished her drink and refused a second. "This feels too much like a funeral. Besides, I have to drive home."

She strode off, businesslike as ever, with just the quiver of her chin giving away her emotional state.

"We don't have to drive. Besides, I like funerals." Gran topped up their glasses.

The bottle was a lot emptier when Laura finally served dinner.

"Do you have anything to rush back for, dear?" Gran asked, as they picked at their salad and pretended to eat quiche.

"Hmm?" she asked vaguely.

"I was wondering whether you could stay a week or so and paint my bedroom." She sighed. "You were right when you said I'd get tired of that pink quickly. I know it's only been three years since you did all that fancy painting in there, and it seems rather wasteful...."

Laura hated the idea of staying anywhere near Laroche now that she and Jack were finished. It was physically painful just being on the same island with him. All she wanted was to slink back to Seattle and lick her wounds. Muzzily, she reviewed her options.

She could do as her grandmother asked, which was the very least a good granddaughter would do. She could plead work piling up in Seattle, which was true enough, and hire someone locally to do her gran's bedroom.

Gran sneezed. What kind of a brute left an aged grandmother when she was ill? Laura gazed at the beloved wrinkled face across the table and smiled mistily. "That's a great idea, Gran. It will give us time to visit." She smiled. "Don't worry. I'll get the paint wholesale, and the labor's free. It will hardly cost anything."

Except the cost to her heart.

LAURA GOT UP EARLY the next morning to fetch her tools and materials out of the McNair House.

The tape had been pulled away from the front doorway, so she was able to convince herself that she wasn't really trespassing by entering the house. For good measure she grabbed her hard hat out of the back of her van.

It was before seven when she let herself into the house and paused in the foyer. The last time she'd been in here... She shuddered at the memory of passion, right there on the floor.

She shuddered again at the memory of its bitter aftermath, and the depressing assurance this morning that she definitely wasn't pregnant. With a sigh, she rubbed her tired eyes, determined to get her stuff and get out as soon as possible. She'd brought a hefty flashlight with her, but the early morning light shining in the windows allowed her to see quite well.

She noticed a book, obviously old and probably valuable, lying in the middle of the third step. What on earth was it doing here? Curious, she picked it up.

Opening the cover, she gasped at the inscription. She sat down on the step, angling the book to get the full light from the window, then began to read.

She brushed tears away as she read about Elizabeth McNair's first year in this house. Her love for her husband and his for her. The birth of their first child, a son, upstairs in the bed that was too big to move out because Albert McNair had had it built right in the bedroom, completing the house around it.

Laura read about the trials of Cook and the other servants, of picnics at the seaside, the worries of a new parent, of pickling and drying and preserving foods for winter. She read about Elizabeth McNair's hopes that her second child would be a girl.

The last entry told of a planned trip back to Boston, where Albert had business to attend to.

I long to return to all the gaiety of society, to my friends and family. I long to present my sturdy young son, John. I am only sorry that my second child will not be born in our very own home. Still, I shall not repine. Albert would have left me behind, but I would not hear of it. How should I bear the long winter and the birth of a child without my Albert by my side? I do not think I shall continue my journal while I am away from home. I shall put this little book by in a secret place and pick it up again when I return. How much I shall have to say!

The rest of the pages were blank, but Laura knew from the county historical records that Elizabeth and Albert had returned. She even knew that the second child had been a girl and that the McNairs went on to raise three more children. Perhaps Elizabeth was too busy to continue her journal once she returned, or maybe she just forgot about it.

Laura hugged the little book to her fiercely. "I won't let them tear down this house, I won't," she whispered.

She replaced the diary carefully on the stairs, feeling that it would be wrong to take it outside these walls.

Tracing the old leather cover with a finger-tip, she wondered how she was going to save this house of love, which had been part of her ever since she could remember.

Time was running out.

She remembered Mrs. Walters telling them about an offer that expired next Friday. What on earth could she do in a little more than a week, with her contract canceled?

Her hand stilled on the book cover.

Suddenly, she snapped her fingers.

It was simple. She'd buy the house herself.

Maybe she couldn't have the whole dream, but she could have part of it. If she couldn't have Jack, at least she could have this special house. She had some money put away, enough for a solid down payment. She could take in roommates or turn the McNair House into a bed-and-breakfast inn. And she was close enough to Seattle that she could still keep her business.

Excitement pumped through her veins. It could work.

The whole idea was impulsive and ludicrous—and Laura knew she was going to do it. It felt right. The house had been waiting for her all these years. Elizabeth's diary as good as proved it.

She ran home to Gran's, only to find the place empty.

That was odd. Her grandmother hadn't mentioned she was going out, and Laura had so wanted to tell her about her idea. Well, she didn't have time to waste. She fixed her face, changed her clothes, grabbed her purse and was out the door. Minutes later she walked into the local real estate office with a bright smile on her face.

"Hi, I'm Laura Kinkaide. I want to buy the old McNair House," she told the startled man sitting reading the newspaper.

"Who doesn't?" he mumbled, scratching his pure-white crew cut. The matching white moustache curled as he smiled and offered Laura a chair.

"I know there's a bid from a developer that expires next Friday. That's why I want to put my offer in as soon as possible."

The old man's eyes were dancing. She supposed he was excited about the commission he would earn if he could get her the property.

"I see. And you're, ah, planning to buy this property alone?" He was looking at her strangely, his eyes still twinkling.

Oh, great. Just my luck. A dinosaur who doesn't believe women should own property. "Yes." She made her voice brisk. "I have quite a successful business, an excellent credit history and a healthy investment portfolio. I'll cash part of that in, of course, for the down payment."

"I see." The man held out his hand. "Jed Hansen. I know your grandmother well. Have you talked to her about this?"

"No, I just decided today."

Jed Hansen's mustache lifted again as he chuckled. "You're not buying a hat, young lady. Would you like to think it over? Talk to someone you trust?"

Really, this guy's attitude was too much. She felt a flush heating her face. "Aren't you supposed to talk me *into* buying property?"

He laughed out loud at that. "I want all my customers to be happy, Miss Kinkaide. You can make mistakes if you rush."

"Thank you. But I've made up my mind."

The newspaper rustled as he folded it carefully and laid it to one side. "Tell you what. I'll start the paperwork for you. You'll need a five-thousand-dollar deposit and a letter from your bank saying they'll lend you the rest of the money. Then, if you still want the house, come back in. I'll have the papers ready for you."

He really was the strangest old guy. He seemed to be laughing at some kind of private joke throughout the whole interview. She thanked him dubiously and left.

She walked the block and a half to the bank, hoping Mary wouldn't treat a lone woman borrowing mortgage money as some kind of joke. She was just reaching forward to open the bank door when it banged into her and Jack came out. He jumped when he saw her and a guilty expression came over his face. As it should.

"Laura, are you all right?"

"Don't worry, Jack. It was a false alarm. I'm fine."

He seemed totally confused. "But the door..."

She raised her gaze skyward and whispered, "I got my period."

Pain flashed in his eyes; she was sure of it. "Did you go and get that pill thing?"

"My private affairs are none of your business." She stuck her nose in the air and stalked past him.

Or tried to.

He grabbed her shoulders and hauled her back, spinning her to face him, his eyes boring into hers. "Did you?"

She opened her mouth to tell him in stronger, more colorful terms to mind his own business, then saw something in his face that made her tell him the simple truth. "No. No, I didn't."

He let her go and his jaw unclenched enough for him to spit out, "I'm sorry." He strode away and Laura was left wondering just what that was all about. If he cared so much, why hadn't he tried a little harder to see her? And more to the point, why was she wasting time watching him walk away? She had business to attend to.

This time she made it through the door to the bank unmolested. When she entered the dim foyer and asked for Mary, no one questioned whether she had an appointment or made her wait all afternoon. She was ushered into the bank manager's tidy office almost immediately. Chalk up another one for small towns.

Mary rose and shook hands, waving Laura to a chair. "I'm so sorry, Laura. Losing the McNair House is a real blow to the community. I suppose you're here about your severance?"

"No. I'm here to buy the McNair House."

Mary made a choking noise. "I...I see."

"Is there spinach stuck in my teeth or something?" Laura ran her tongue over her front teeth to check.

Mary squinted at her in surprise. "I don't think so."

"Everywhere I go today, people keep smirking when they look at me. You, the real-estate agent...I don't get it. Is it my hair? A button undone?" She glanced down, but her buttons seemed in place, her fly was zipped up all the way. She looked questioningly at Mary. "What?"

"You look fine, Laura. I was, um, thinking about something else. So you want to buy the McNair House—good for you. I wish I could afford it. I think it's a very shrewd investment."

Laura nodded. "I've got a pretty good down payment, but I need approval for a mortgage before I submit a bid."

Mary pulled her keyboard closer and started tapping away. "The city finance committee is meeting next Friday to review all bids. They don't necessarily have to take the highest one, you know. They have the discretion to decide which bid is best for the city. The fact that you plan to restore an historic building rather than demolish it will work in your favor. You might also consider offering to open the house to the public on certain days of the year, for instance. That might help swing the committee in your favor even if the other bids are higher."

"Other bids? I thought there was just one."

Mary kept her eyes fixed on the computer screen. "I'm speaking hypothetically, of course. Here we are. I've pulled up a mortgage application. I'll ask you a series of questions, and we should be able to confirm your mortgage by late tomorrow, possibly earlier. Is that acceptable?"

"Yes. Thanks."

"Let's start with your current address."

11

LAURA DROPPED HER BID OFF at city hall on Thursday. She'd included the price she was willing to pay, a list of improvements she planned to make, even a few of the interior sketches she'd already completed.

She wrote a fawning letter about how important McNair House was as a community landmark and how she planned to offer the home for charity events and hold open houses during Christmas and the tourist season.

After she'd returned from making her mortgage application, she'd decided not to tell Gran about her plans, after all. What a terrific surprise it would be.

Laura was amazed at how few qualms she had now that she'd decided to buy the house. Every time she looked at her grandmother she felt a surge of pleasure, knowing she would be there to look after the older woman she loved so much. Even the prospect of living on the same island as Jack didn't scare her anymore. In the past few weeks, she had finally grown up.

She and Gran spent days together choosing paint colors, new curtains and bedding. Then Laura hauled on her overalls and painted the bedroom and adjoining bathroom in soft blue, with a hand-painted wisteria border.

In the evenings, they sat and talked over tea and

Gran's famous oatmeal cookies. One night they managed to get hold of Laura's mother at the commune in New Mexico where she was living with her latest boyfriend. She promised to come up and visit, real soon.

Maybe because she spent so much of the week inside Gran's house, or maybe because he was avoiding her, Laura didn't see Jack at all.

Which was just fine by her.

Friday, she washed the windows in Gran's bedroom and hung the new curtains they'd picked out, while she tried to ignore the butterflies in her stomach. Twice she ran to the top of the stairs and called down, "Was that the phone?"

The second time, Gran stomped to the bottom of the stairs and called up, "There's a phone in the bedroom. It was working yesterday. I believe it's still in order."

Once the bedroom was completely finished, and her grandmother had duly admired the new look, Laura had nothing much to do but wait and plan how she would spring her surprise.

"I wish you'd get your head out of the clouds, Laura," the old woman finally snapped. "I said I won't be home for lunch. That doesn't call for thanks."

"Sorry, Gran. I was thinking about something else."

"Like when you're going back to Seattle?"

"What? Oh, I'm not sure. I thought I'd stay on a few more days, if that's okay with you."

Gran raised her eyebrows. "I'm delighted. I just thought you had jobs waiting."

"I do. But I'd like to spend some more time here." She couldn't wait to tell Gran just how much time she was going to be spending in Laroche.

IT WAS THE MAYOR who called Laura Friday afternoon. "Hello, Miss Kinkaide. It's Edward Marks here."

"Yes, sir." Her heart pounded with excitement. This was it. Her new life was about to start. She had saved the McNair House single-handedly.

"I'm sorry to inform you your bid was not successful." His cheerfully impersonal voice sounded like the weatherman's.

"What did you say?" Surely she hadn't heard him right.

"I'm sorry, Miss Kinkaide. You didn't get McNair House."

She felt as if he'd slapped her. "You mean you sold it to the developer? But he's just going to tear it down and build condos! You can't let that happen."

"I'm not at liberty to discuss the details. The buyer has asked the committee to keep his or her identity confidential. An announcement will be made at next week's council meeting. Good day, Miss Kinkaide."

He hung up before she could get her mouth to move.

What were they thinking of? Mary had said they would take other factors into consideration. It just didn't make any sense. Laura wished it wasn't Gran's afternoon to play bridge. That mayor's backside needed another good paddling.

Well, maybe Laura could talk some sense into him. She had a right to know why her bid wasn't good enough.

And if it had anything to do with her being a woman...

Determined to confront Mr. Marks at her best, she showered, took time over her hair and makeup and dressed in a cream cotton skirt and a lacy lavender sweater. Gathering her complete portfolio of designs for the McNair House and the preapproved mortgage documents, she jumped into her van and roared downtown.

She'd make somebody, somewhere, listen to her, show them all her ideas. She'd raise her offer, beg and plead if necessary. But she was going to save that house.

As she marched toward the mayor's office, she spotted a familiar figure marching toward her from the opposite direction. He had a briefcase in his hands. They almost collided at the entrance to city hall.

Jack's face was creased in an angry frown. "What are you doing here?"

"I'm here on business," she snapped back, furious that she was still so crazy about this man who made a habit of stomping all over her heart. He could at least pretend to be happy to see her. "What are you doing here?"

"Business."

"Well, mine's urgent." She tried to elbow past him into city hall.

"So's mine." He neatly hip-checked her out of the way and stomped through the doorway.

She was right behind him. "I can't believe you did that. If Gran saw you she'd—"

"This is business, honey. No gender biasing, remember?" His anger melted and his eyes glinted with suppressed humor.

"Please, Jack. My business really is important."

"More important than trying to buy the McNair House?"

Laura's jaw dropped. Suddenly all the funny looks and snickering she'd put up with when she was getting her bid together made sense. She'd been bidding against Jack.

"Don't tell me you were the successful bidder?" He'd already stolen her heart; now he'd as good as stolen the house from under her, too.

"No, my bid was rejected." The angry frown descended once more. "And I'm damn well going to find out why. I'll see you later." He walked toward the reception counter.

Laura followed.

He turned to her. "Look, I'm sorry, Laura," he said softly. "I know how much that house means to you. I'm not giving up. But, please, let me handle this."

"I told you, I have my own business at city hall," she informed him. "Like finding out why *my* bid was rejected."

It was Jack's turn to drop his jaw. Then his eyes crinkled.

"You and I were bidding against each other?"

Laura bit her lip. She wished he wouldn't look at her that way. It made her forget all the excellent arguments she'd marshaled for her upcoming confrontation with Mr. Marks. "Yeah."

They were a couple of feet from the desk, and he was still gazing at her in amazement. "But what about your life in Seattle? Your business...?"

"We close in ten minutes. If you want something, Jack, you'd better get moving," the woman at the scarred oak counter announced.

"Hi, Linda. We'd like to see Ed."

"I suppose it can't keep till Monday?" She sounded resigned but hopeful.

"Nope."

The clerk stepped through a doorway behind her, then reappeared. "Come on in," she said, holding the door open with her foot until they'd passed through.

Laura had met Edward Marks at the committee meeting, and he'd reminded her of a schoolteacher. He had the earnest look of a scholar with his thick glasses and ill-fitting sports jacket.

He glanced at her, then at Jack, and the twinkle Laura was beginning to associate with the whole bidding process was in his eyes. "So, you two know about each other."

"We just found out," Jack said curtly. "Look, Ed. There's something funny going on around here. Everybody in town wants to save the McNair House. You have two perfectly good bids to keep it, Laura's and mine. Why the hell are you selling an historic landmark to a developer who'll knock it down?"

The twinkle in the mayor's eyes disappeared. He sighed and said, "I wish you'd wait till next week. I've explained to both of you I can't discuss the details of the successful bid."

"But we have a right to know—"

"No, you don't. The house won't be knocked down this weekend, for heaven's sake. Wait until you have all the information, then you're welcome to take any action you deem appropriate. I'm sorry, but until next week, I can't discuss this."

They argued themselves hoarse, but it was hopeless. Edward Marks was polite. He admired Laura's drawings. He showed genuine interest in Jack's plan to donate the rose garden to the city as a park—and darn, but she wished she'd thought of that! Yet the mayor wouldn't be goaded into telling them anything.

The woman in the front office made a noisy production out of locking up, but Jack didn't seem to hear the obvious hint. He was fighting for the house as though it were the most important thing in the world.

Laura watched him, so tall and proud and confident, and all the anger seeped out of her. What was a house but a shell? It was what went on inside that was important. There were other houses. The important thing was that she was home to stay. And maybe with time, she and Jack could make a fresh start. Anything was possible.

"Excuse me," she interrupted. "I'm leaving now. Sorry to bother you, Mr. Marks."

"Anytime, Miss Kinkaide," the tired-looking mayor assured her.

"Bye, Jack," she said, and quickly left the room.

When she reached her van, she realized Jack had followed her. He waited until she'd stowed her portfolio. "Laura," he said gently. "Walk with me."

She nodded, feeling her heart leap when she heard the appeal in his voice.

He leaned past her to put his briefcase beside her portfolio, and his arm brushed hers—just the tiniest whisper of a touch, but the impact on her senses was electric. He turned his head to stare at her and she knew he'd felt it, too, the surge of awareness that had her pulses thrumming. Making eye contact only increased the chaos overtaking her nervous system.

The expression on his face was intense as he raised his hands to grip her shoulders. "This isn't over. I'm going to that council meeting next week to talk some sense into the village idiots who run this town—"

"Good night, Jack, Miss Kinkaide."

As one, Jack and Laura jerked their heads in the direction of Edward Marks's voice. The man was right behind them, carefully unlocking the door of his blue sedan.

"Uh, night, Ed."

"Good night, Mr. Marks."

The mayor gave an ironic little wave as he slid behind the wheel.

"Well, that'll sure help my case," Jack muttered, while Laura shut and locked her van, stifling a helpless grin.

A crazy idea was forming in her mind, that maybe, just maybe, he wasn't only after the old house.

THEY WALKED TOGETHER down the quiet sidewalk, past the shops and restaurants that fronted the seaside. Laura couldn't look at Jack. Hope and fear warred within her as she waited for him to speak, but he took his time, shoving his hands in his pockets and kicking a pebble ahead of him.

Finally, he said, "Why do you want the house?" His voice sounded strained. She turned and found him staring at her, his face eager.

She bit her lip and kept walking. "This is my home. Gran's here. I can run my business from Whidbey. There are all kinds of historic properties in the area. And I could still do projects in Seattle. It's not that far."

She wanted to make certain he knew she wasn't hanging around just for him.

"I could take in room-mates if I need help with the mortgage," she continued. "Maybe even turn the place into a b and b when I finish decorating it. Once I saw that diary I couldn't bear to let the house go. Thanks for leaving it out for me to find." Her heart was hammering. She stared ahead down the deserted sidewalk. "How about you? Why do you want it?"

"I was hoping to bribe you with the house," he said at last.

"Pardon?" She turned her head to gape at him, and saw that his face was set in grim lines.

He kept walking. Now he was the one staring straight ahead, afraid to look at her. She scrambled to catch up as he said, "I want to marry you. I thought maybe if the house was part of the package, you might consider it. I know how much you love that house." He swallowed. "I blew it. I'm sorry."

"Oh, Jack..."

The pebble skipped ahead as he kicked it, watching its progress through narrowed eyes. "At first I just wanted our friendship back. Then it got so I couldn't stop thinking about you. I knew you'd go back to Seattle after a few months, but I figured I could handle an affair. It was better than nothing. But I was wrong, it's no good. I figured out the other night I was in love with you."

"But, Jack—"

"No, let me finish. I have to get this out." His voice was husky. "I didn't slip up on purpose. God knows, I don't want to go down that road again. But after you ran out that night, I went home and just sat for a while, figuring things out. I finally figured out that I did want you to be pregnant with my child. I just wanted you to be happy about it."

Laura was having trouble seeing through the tears in her eyes, which was how she came to trip.

Jack caught her before she fell, then didn't seem able to let go of her. He was gazing into her eyes with such tenderness that her tears spilled over.

"I'd love to have your child," she managed to gasp, smiling and wiping her eyes at the same time. "I wish I *had* been pregnant."

His lips came down and claimed hers as her eyes overflowed again. She was laughing and crying and kissing at the same time.

She almost fainted from lack of breath.

He lifted his head and hugged her to him. "I've missed you so much. Right from the beginning when you first left. After I messed up so badly, I missed having my best friend to talk to. So many times I've wanted to pick up the phone and call you."

"Really?"

He nodded. "But the few times you came to town you avoided me. Then we got the chance to work together and I hoped we could be friends again. I never dreamed *this* could happen." He kissed her again to emphasize his meaning.

"Neither did I." She cupped his cheeks with her palms, relishing the love and tenderness she saw in the depths of his blue eyes. The breeze tossed his dark-blond hair across his forehead and she reached up to smooth it back. It was a possessive gesture. A wifely gesture.

"You were right all those years ago," he said. "You weren't too young for me. It was me who was too young for you."

"We've both grown up a lot," she agreed.

A lone pedestrian emerged from a shop and strolled toward them.

"Keep walking or we'll have the whole town gossiping about us," Laura warned, knowing the best-kept secret lasted mere minutes in Laroche.

"Good," said Jack, taking her hand firmly in his. He let her drag him along with her, and she let him keep her hand in his.

"I thought, after..." She felt herself coloring. "After we didn't use anything that night—I felt so rejected. Like you didn't want me or a child."

He pulled her back into his arms, heedless of the gossips. "No! How could you think that? I just didn't want to trap you into marrying me. Believe me, it doesn't work," he said bitterly.

"I...I do want children," she said softly.

"I want more children, too. I think you'll make a wonderful mother. The only thing Cory was right about was that Sara needs a mother. Are you willing to take that on?"

Laura smiled, letting the happiness that was swelling her heart spill over again. "I like Sara very much. Once I get to know her better I know I'm going to love her. We'll be a happy family, I'm sure of it."

"If love and hard work are enough, I'm sure of it, too."

She sighed, and didn't protest when he put his arm around her waist and pulled her close. So what if the whole town found out they were in love? "Who do we tell first? Gran or Sara?"

Jack grinned the wolfish grin that made Laura quiver. "I already packed Sara off to her friend's for the night. You see, I was planning on surprising you with an engagement ring and the McNair House. I already have dinner reservations at a great little place I know up island."

"Pretty cocky, aren't you?" Laura teased.

"Let's just say...hopeful."

She traced his upper lip with her index finger. "Does this little place cater to overnight guests?"

He took her finger into his mouth and bit gently, his tongue hot and delicious against the sensitive fingertip. "Now who's cocky?" From her finger, his mouth moved to her thumb and then finally to her lips. "Now you mention it, they might just have a room tonight with my name on it."

Just the thought of the two of them, alone together for the night, had her heart fluttering. How she'd missed his loving. His hand was warm and possessive around her waist and she couldn't wait to feel it on her naked flesh. "So you really want to marry me."

"Mm-hmm."

"I wonder how Cory will feel...having me take her place...."

He shook his head. "You won't take her place. Her idea of being a mother is flitting into town once in a while with presents. She can still do that. And Sara can still have her annual birthday trip to see her mom. But

Sara will also have a woman in her life every day to help her and guide her. That's what she really needs."

"I'll try my best."

He cleared his throat. "I've already talked to the real-estate agent about putting my place up for sale. If we can't have the McNair House, I want to build you a house. On the ocean, if you like."

She was so relieved he didn't expect her to live in Cory's old house she couldn't resist teasing him. "Can I have one just like Chip's? I still want to do a harem bedroom."

"We'll build anything you want if you're sure you'll marry me."

She smiled up at him and let him see everything she felt. "I've wanted to marry you since I got my first training bra." Then she tugged at his hand. "Let's tell Gran."

As it turned out, they didn't have to tell that wise old woman anything. They walked into the house, deliberately not touching. Gran took one look at them and snorted. "Well, it's about time."

"Oh. I'm so happy." Laura threw her arms around the frail figure and squeezed.

"Leave me a rib or two unbroken, girl. I plan to dance at your wedding," Gran scolded, but her eyes were teary.

Then it was Jack's turn to hug her. "I'm a lucky man," he said huskily.

"Yes, you are," Gran agreed. "You're both lucky. You've spent a lot of years trying to deny the obvious. You two were meant for each other. I'm glad you finally came to your senses. You'll find champagne in the fridge, Jack. We'll have it in the living room."

The living room. Jack and Laura exchanged glances. The living room was dusted and polished once a week and used about twice a year. This was a real occasion.

"Why have you got champagne in the fridge, Gran? Don't tell me you have 'the sight.'"

"Don't be cheeky, young lady. Mildred Aspick phoned me an hour ago from the Seaside Boutique. After the way you've been carrying on in public with my granddaughter, Jack, you'll *have* to marry her."

"I intend to." His promise floated back from the kitchen.

"Good, I have a wedding present for you."

The champagne was French and expensive. Jack and Laura exchanged amazed glances again. "I'd like to propose a toast," Gran said, raising her champagne flute.

Jack raised his glass, smiling at Laura with warmth in his eyes and promises that made her eager to get to that bed-and-breakfast inn.

"I wish you the kind of love that builds with time. The kind of love that's worth working for—and fighting for, if you have to. It's the only kind worth having. To Jack and Laura." Gran raised her glass at them and sipped.

Laura's future husband mouthed "to us" and drank. Out of the corner of her eye, she watched Gran raise her glass in a tiny salute to Grandpa's picture. A lump formed in Laura's throat as she realized how indebted she was to Gran and Grandpa for the example they'd set her of married life.

She sipped the cold, frothy champagne and made a silent toast to another couple who'd gone before her and taught her about building a successful marriage—Elizabeth and Albert McNair.

Gran retrieved a plain brown, legal-size envelope from the table beside her and handed it to Laura. "Your wedding present."

The envelope crackled loudly in the still room. Puzzled, Laura removed the single sheet of paper, scanned it rapidly and felt her eyes bug out of her head.

Too shocked to speak, she silently passed the letter to Jack, who took it from her nerveless hand and read aloud. "'Dear Mrs. McMurtry, It is my pleasure to inform you that the committee has accepted your bid to purchase the property known as McNair House....'"

His voice petered out, then Jack raised his eyes to stare at Gran. "You were the one who bought the McNair House?" he almost shouted. "But how...?" He stopped, clearly not knowing how to go on.

"He means, how could you possibly afford it, Gran?" Laura crossed the room to kneel at her grandmother's feet and take her gnarled hand. "This is very sweet, but you must have sold everything...we can't let you..."

Gran chuckled—a deep, contented belly laugh. "I'm not one to brag, but I'm a very wealthy woman, dear." Her grandmother paused a moment, enjoying their astonishment. "I've been investing in the stock market since your mother was a baby." She sipped her champagne. "It's been a very lucrative hobby."

Seeing both her listeners were still paralyzed with shock, she continued, "Of course, I have everything I want. I give most of my money to charity these days. But it's nice to be able to buy an extravagant gift for a beloved granddaughter and her fiancé."

Laura stared at her grandmother as though she'd never seen her before. "I thought you just read all that stuff about orange juice futures and stock offerings. I had no idea you were investing."

Her grandmother snorted. "What's the fun in that? The toughest part was keeping it a secret. You know what gossip is like in this town." Gran rolled her eyes as though she personally had never stooped to such depths. Ha!

"So that's why Ed wouldn't tell anyone who the successful bidder was," Jack said.

The old woman nodded. "And they'll never find out. Next week, it will be announced that you two are the new owners of McNair House. And it will be the truth."

"You're the best grandmother anyone ever had," Laura said.

"And the best fairy godmother," Jack agreed.

A SOFT, EARLY MORNING breeze brought a faint tang of the ocean to tease Laura's nose. She snuggled deeper under the faded quilt, enjoying the familiar warm weight of Jack's arm curled round her body. The fingers of his relaxed hand just touched her breast. She shifted slightly, filling his curled palm with her eager flesh, rubbing the bud of her nipple back and forth.

His fingers closed obligingly and began to knead and tantalize her while he burrowed his face into her nape, rubbing the sensitive skin of her neck with his stubbly cheek. He kissed and nuzzled until she turned to him in laughing surrender.

"Didn't you get your fill last night?" she teased.

"I have it on good authority that I married a sex addict. Don't tell me the honeymoon cured you?" He was trying to look hurt, while his fingers traced their way over her body, touching her in a way that always aroused her.

She looked into the eyes of her brand-new husband, and knew she had found happiness for life. "I don't think I'll ever be cured," she said huskily, and leaned over to kiss him.

With the last of the renovations finished, Laura had spent the days leading up to her wedding back on the ladder, stenciling cabbage roses. Jack had repaired the master bedroom with such skill it was impossible to tell the old part of the room from the new.

As she glanced around the special room, she felt as though Elizabeth McNair was smiling down on her, happy that this home was once again a house of love. Laura glanced at the mantel, where the diary held pride of place, and smiled back.

For now, she and Jack had the house to themselves, but Sara would be back in a few days from a visit with her mom, who hadn't taken the news of Jack's choice of bride all that well. It was Sara herself who'd finally convinced Cory that Laura was the right person for both her and her dad.

Sara's room, just down the hall from the master bedroom, was still not decorated. She'd begged Laura to wait until she got back so they could work on it together. It was a project they were both excited about. Jack's daughter had been almost as thrilled about the marriage as Laura's grandmother. Not only had the crafty old woman been the mysterious philanthropist, but she'd arranged for Jack and Laura to work together in the first place.

But Gran wasn't the only one taking credit for match-making. Stan had sent the horsehair parlor set he'd picked up at auction as a wedding present, along with a card that said, "I told you he was the one."

Laura chuckled aloud. "You know, everyone keeps telling us we were meant for each other. I can't believe it took us so long to figure it out."

"Was it worth the wait?" Jack patted the heirloom quilt significantly, a grinning question in his eyes.

"I haven't decided yet," she claimed, grinning back, and pulled him down for another kiss. The big old bed hardly creaked as they made slow, langorous love, beginning one more marriage in the house that love built.

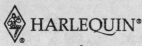

Harlequin truly does
make any time special....
This year we are celebrating
weddings in style!

A Walk Down the Aisle
WEDDING CELEBRATION

To help us celebrate, we want you to tell us how wearing the Harlequin wedding gown will make your wedding day special. As the grand prize, Harlequin will offer one lucky bride the chance to **"Walk Down the Aisle"** in the Harlequin wedding gown!

There's more...

For her honeymoon, she and her groom will spend five nights at the **Hyatt Regency Maui.** As part of this five-night honeymoon at the hotel renowned for its romantic attractions, the couple will enjoy a candlelit dinner for two in Swan Court, a sunset sail on the hotel's catamaran, and duet spa treatments.

A HYATT RESORT AND SPA®   Maui • Molokai • Lenai

To enter, please write, in, 250 words or less, how wearing the Harlequin wedding gown will make your wedding day special. The entry will be judged based on its emotionally compelling nature, its originality and creativity, and its sincerity. This contest is open to Canadian and U.S. residents only and to those who are 18 years of age and older. There is no purchase necessary to enter. Void where prohibited. See further contest rules attached. Please send your entry to:

Walk Down the Aisle Contest

In Canada	In U.S.A.
P.O. Box 637	P.O. Box 9076
Fort Erie, Ontario	3010 Walden Ave.
L2A 5X3	Buffalo, NY 14269-9076

You can also enter by visiting www.eHarlequin.com
Win the Harlequin wedding gown and the vacation of a lifetime!
The deadline for entries is October 1, 2001.

HARLEQUIN®
Makes any time special®

PHWDACONT1

HARLEQUIN WALK DOWN THE AISLE TO MAUI CONTEST 1197
OFFICIAL RULES
NO PURCHASE NECESSARY TO ENTER

1. To enter, follow directions published in the offer to which you are responding. Contest begins April 2, 2001, and ends on October 1, 2001. Method of entry may vary. Mailed entries must be postmarked by October 1, 2001, and received by October 8, 2001.

2. Contest entry may be, at times, presented via the Internet, but will be restricted solely to residents of certain geographic areas that are disclosed on the Web site. To enter via the Internet, if permissible, access the Harlequin Web site (www.eHarlequin.com) and follow the directions displayed online. Online entries must be received by 11:59 p.m. E.S.T. on October 1, 2001.

   In lieu of submitting an entry online, enter by mail by hand-printing (or typing) on an 8½" x 11" plain piece of paper, your name, address (including zip code), Contest number/name and in 250 words or fewer, why winning a Harlequin wedding dress would make your wedding day special. Mail via first-class mail to: Harlequin Walk Down the Aisle Contest 1197, (in the U.S.) P.O. Box 9076, 3010 Walden Avenue, Buffalo, NY 14269-9076, (in Canada) P.O. Box 637, Fort Erie, Ontario L2A 5X3, Canada.

   Limit one entry per person, household address and e-mail address. Online and/or mailed entries received from persons residing in geographic areas in which Internet entry is not permissible will be disqualified.

3. Contests will be judged by a panel of members of the Harlequin editorial, marketing and public relations staff based on the following criteria:

   - Originality and Creativity—50%
   - Emotionally Compelling—25%
   - Sincerity—25%

   In the event of a tie, duplicate prizes will be awarded. Decisions of the judges are final.

4. All entries become the property of Torstar Corp. and will not be returned. No responsibility is assumed for lost, late, illegible, incomplete, inaccurate, nondelivered or misdirected mail or misdirected e-mail, for technical, hardware or software failures of any kind, lost or unavailable network connections, or failed, incomplete, garbled or delayed computer transmission or any human error which may occur in the receipt or processing of the entries in this Contest.

5. Contest open only to residents of the U.S. (except Puerto Rico) and Canada, who are 18 years of age or older, and is void wherever prohibited by law; all applicable laws and regulations apply. Any litigation within the Province of Quebec respecting the conduct or organization of a publicity contest may be submitted to the Régie des alcools, des courses et des jeux for a ruling. Any litigation respecting the awarding of a prize may be submitted to the Régie des alcools, des courses et des jeux only for the purpose of helping the parties reach a settlement. Employees and immediate family members of Torstar Corp. and D. L. Blair, Inc., their affiliates, subsidiaries and all other agencies, entities and persons connected with the use, marketing or conduct of this Contest are not eligible to enter. Taxes on prizes are the sole responsibility of winners. Acceptance of any prize offered constitutes permission to use winner's name, photograph or other likeness for the purposes of advertising, trade and promotion on behalf of Torstar Corp., its affiliates and subsidiaries without further compensation to the winner, unless prohibited by law.

6. Winners will be determined no later than November 15, 2001, and will be notified by mail. Winners will be required to sign and return an Affidavit of Eligibility form within 15 days after winner notification. Noncompliance within that time period may result in disqualification and an alternative winner may be selected. Winners of trip must execute a Release of Liability prior to ticketing and must possess required travel documents (e.g. passport, photo ID) where applicable. Trip must be completed by November 2002. No substitution of prize permitted by winner. Torstar Corp. and D. L. Blair, Inc., their parents, affiliates, and subsidiaries are not responsible for errors in printing or electronic presentation of Contest, entries and/or game pieces. In the event of printing or other errors which may result in unintended prize values or duplication of prizes, all affected game pieces or entries shall be null and void. If for any reason the Internet portion of the Contest is not capable of running as planned, including infection by computer virus, bugs, tampering, unauthorized intervention, fraud, technical failures, or any other causes beyond the control of Torstar Corp. which corrupt or affect the administration, secrecy, fairness, integrity or proper conduct of the Contest, Torstar Corp. reserves the right, at its sole discretion, to disqualify any individual who tampers with the entry process and to cancel, terminate, modify or suspend the Contest or the Internet portion thereof. In the event of a dispute regarding an online entry, the entry will be deemed submitted by the authorized holder of the e-mail account submitted at the time of entry. Authorized account holder is defined as the natural person who is assigned to an e-mail address by an Internet access provider, online service provider or other organization that is responsible for arranging e-mail address for the domain associated with the submitted e-mail address. **Purchase or acceptance of a product offer does not improve your chances of winning.**

7. Prizes: (1) Grand Prize—A Harlequin wedding dress (approximate retail value: $3,500) and a 5-night/6-day honeymoon trip to Maui, HI, including round-trip air transportation provided by Maui Visitors Bureau from Los Angeles International Airport (winner is responsible for transportation to and from Los Angeles International Airport) and a Harlequin Romance Package, including hotel accomodations (double occupancy) at the Hyatt Regency Maui Resort and Spa, dinner for (2) two at Swan Court, a sunset sail on Kiele V and a spa treatment for the winner (approximate retail value: $4,000); (5) Five runner-up prizes of a $1000 gift certificate to selected retail outlets to be determined by Sponsor (retail value $1000 ea.). Prizes consist of only those items listed as part of the prize. Limit one prize per person. All prizes are valued in U.S. currency.

8. For a list of winners (available after December 17, 2001) send a self-addressed, stamped envelope to: Harlequin Walk Down the Aisle Contest 1197 Winners, P.O. Box 4200 Blair, NE 68009-4200 or you may access the www.eHarlequin.com Web site through January 15, 2002.

Contest sponsored by Torstar Corp., P.O. Box 9042, Buffalo, NY 14269-9042, U.S.A.

*Three sizzling love stories
by today's hottest writers
can be found in...*

Midnight Fantasies....

Feel the heat!

Available July 2001

MYSTERY LOVER—*Vicki Lewis Thompson*

When an unexpected storm hits, rancher Jonas Garfield
takes cover in a nearby cave...and finds himself seduced
senseless by an enigmatic temptress who refuses to tell him
her name. All he knows is that this sexy woman wants him.
And for Jonas, that's enough—for now....

AFTER HOURS—*Stephanie Bond*

Michael Pierce has always considered costume shop
owner Rebecca Valentine no more than an associate—
until he drops by her shop one night and witnesses the
mousy wallflower's transformation into a seductive siren.
Suddenly he's desperate to know her much better.
But which woman is the real Rebecca?

SHOW AND TELL—*Kimberly Raye*

A naughty lingerie party. A forbidden fantasy. When Texas
bad boy Dallas Jericho finds a slip of paper left over from
the party, he is surprised—and aroused—to discover that he
is good girl Laney Merriweather's wildest fantasy. So what
can he do but show the lady what she's been missing....